ASHVAMEDHA

THE GAME OF POWER

ASHVAMEDHA

THE GAME OF POWER

APARNA SINHA

Srishti
PUBLISHERS & DISTRIBUTORS

Srishti Publishers & Distributors
Registered Office: N-16, C.R. Park
New Delhi – 110 019
Corporate Office: 212A, Peacock Lane
Shahpur Jat, New Delhi – 110 049
editorial@srishtipublishers.com

First published by
Srishti Publishers & Distributors in 2016

To Daddy.

Acknowledgements

Today, if I am able to write this acknowledgment, it is because of some people who always motivated me to dream. *Dream big!*

Let me start by thanking my husband, Vishal Makhija, for being a strong force in my life, for all the encouragement and support, for loving me unconditionally, and for giving me the greatest joy of my life – our son, Zayan. He is a wonderful husband and an even better father.

Thanks to my mother, Meera Sinha, for not only giving me genes for writing (she is a published author herself) but also inspiring me to write every day, for the love and care. She is a phenomenal woman with extraordinary intelligence; she is my role model.

Big thanks to my mother-in-law, Veena Makhija, for accepting me for who I am; for standing by my life choices, all through these years, for all the prayers for my well being. She is truly an inspiration.

I would like to thank the very professional team of Srishti for trusting my story, for the support and guidance and for being very patient with me, throughout. They are delightful people to work with.

Thanks to Pinaki Da for the cover design and insightful sessions on graphic novels. He is indeed the best.

Also thanking:

My family, both the sides – Sinhas and Makhijas.

My friends from all over the world.

And finally, the authors of numerous papers on economy and world politics I referred to while writing the book.

I have manipulated truth
Veiled it, snubbed it
I didn't let you see it
I propagated a lie
Enforced it, inducted it
And you believed in it

I only made your God
Pure and white
And let you pray him
I moulded the Satan
In Dark and Black
Make you fear him

I controlled, I manoeuvred
I turned reality into illusion
I morphed good into evil
I made rules for you to follow
I scripted your destiny
I defined you

I am the instructor of your thoughts
Driver of your cynicism
I am the master of your life
Writer of your fate
I am your belief
I am the Power

Part-I

Thou hast come into being by the toil; the work of the gods thou art the way of holy order. With the Vasus, the gods, as deity, with the Gayatri metre I yoke thee, with the spring season as oblation I consecrate thee.

—Yajur Veda, Taittiriya Samhita, Khand VII 1.18

2

Barely a few kilometres from Thar, a small village of Bikampur had turned into a burning furnace. It was afternoon and roads were deserted. A bored ten-year-old boy, indifferent to the outside climatic condition, sneaked from his kuccha house and began playing silently with a stick that he had picked up from the street. He ran aimlessly on a barren land, beating every inanimate object on his way. It was a useless exercise and it only made him tired and long for a companion; there was nobody. Parched and dejected, he finally stopped and began beating the dried leaves of a small shrub near him. Although not knowing why, he kept doing that till he heard a deafening blast. Startled, he instinctively looked towards his village. It was safe.

He scanned his surroundings. Finally, he saw a ball of fire falling rapidly from the sky. He must have gone deaf, temporarily, because only after a few seconds he heard an ear-splitting sound as he saw the helicopter in the sky bursting into flames and plummeting down. It crashed with a loud thud, splattering hot pieces of metal all around. A small iron piece that landed just near his feet snapped him out of the shock. He finally breathed and ran towards his village.

The villagers heard the sound too and they all rushed towards the helicopter – the heap of metal still on fire. Overcoming their anxieties and severity of conditions, they began pouring water on the fire. Water was scarce there, but they knew there could be people inside; empathy overpowered practicality. Water touched the metal and became smoke instantly.

As the fire subdued and the thick smoke rose up, chance of any life existence in the machine thinned down to zero. While the dejected villagers began returning to their homes, the boy's father looked deep into the smoke, his eyes watering, just to think of his only son's narrow escape. He stood there for some time, gave the machine a final look, pursed his lips and made a call.

"Allah be praised – it's done."

♌

Hades got up late today, *again*. It was eleven in the morning and he hardly felt rested. His eyes were heavy and his body racked. He was so tired as if he had not slept at all. Physically, he might be a mess but his heart was as light as a feather. He slumped on a tattered armchair, switched on the TV and quickly surfed all the news channels; they were all running the 'breaking news' –

'Death of Union Minister Ashok Kumar Nandi in a mysterious helicopter crash'

He watched silently as various pictures of the crumpled and burnt helicopter kept flashing from different angles. A petite news correspondent was speaking rapidly with forced voice modulation –

'The reverend minister was travelling to Mumbai for a political function when this unfortunate accident happened. Police is suspecting rotor malfunction. Along with Mr Nandi, the deceased include his secretary and pilots of the aircraft

'It's a tragedy and the entire nation mourns the death of its beloved minister. The honorable President and Prime Minister have also expressed their grief…'

He muted the TV and leaned back, as faces of all those in power appeared on the screen, expressing loss. Fake visages. His eyes scanned the dry paint on the ceiling – *It's a tragedy and the entire nation mourns.* He chuckled; there were too many lies in that single line.

℈

Ashwin Jamwal, president of the Nationalistic Party, paced around his office while talking on the phone. It was the fifth call in the past one hour. Only a week back he was named the party president, but he didn't feel like a fresher at all.

He disconnected the call and looked at the people in the room. Their seats signified their ranks and positions in the party. Young party members of varied grades were sitting on the white plastic chairs that lined the walls of the room, while the party vice president, I.M. Raathi, and secretary, Suresh Armugham were sitting on cushioned chairs across his seat.

"That's a tragedy indeed," Ashwin said, pointing at the device in his hand. He was referring to the sudden death of Ashok Kumar Nandi. Raathi nodded solemnly and silence followed. Except for the clanking of glasses, as the peon passed the long awaited tea to each member, there was no other sound in the room. Not even a whisper.

"But he was a bastard!" Ashwin said under his breath. The party members, who heard him, chuckled loudly. Raathi nodded again while Armugham kept a stoic expressionless face.

When one sees Suresh Armugham for the first time, one would think that he is angry. Eyes red, eyebrows cringed, no smile or sign of any emotion behind his perfectly trimmed moustache. With time people learnt that he wasn't angry; his face was expressionless.

"This man has been a parasite of the first order," Ashwin continued, "Leech saala! Sucked the blood out of the whole system."

"And money too," somebody added from behind.

Ashwin smiled and resumed, "Politicians like Nandi are the ones who spoil the name of politics and government in the eyes of the people! They spoil the name of the country in the eyes of the world. It's because of people like him we are condemned by the global media; we have become the butt of jokes. We have lost our credibility; global sports associations, alliance organizations, they all look down upon us. But who cares?" He paused and drank his tea in one gulp. "While my heart goes for the family, I don't think his death is a loss for the nation," he added. Some party members chuckled.

His phone buzzed again. He leaned forward and checked. An unknown number. He turned and gave it to his secretary. "It looks like a call from the media, to get my comments on Nandi's death and I have nothing good to say. Please deal with it." The secretary nodded and left with his phone.

"So did they find out the reason for the accident?" Ashwin asked no one in particular.

"Ille. No," spoke Armugham in his thick South Indian accent. "Some technical glitch is what they are saying, but the Centre is demanding a thorough CBI investigation. They think it's the opposition's ploy to kill their strongest leader a few months before the elections."

'Strongest leader?' I.M. Raathi raised an eyebrow

"And most precious leader as well," replied Armugham, his face still taut, though it was a sarcastic remark

I.M. Raathi burst into laughter. "If I am to believe my sources, the party was not planning to contest him from any constituency this year. They were silently planning to get rid of him. He may have been an important member earlier, but recently he was not even involved in any key decision. He used to bring lots of funds through his connections with the Thandi Group." Raathi winked at Armugham slyly and added, "but lately even that had stopped. Nandi was useless and you know what does *realpolitik* says about dead weight. Who knows, it could be his own party behind his death." He shrugged.

"The thing is you cannot even trust the investigation agencies in India." Armugham sighed.

Ashwin gave him an acceptance smile and asked, "So the biggies are fighting again?"

"It's good news, Ashwin. It will only make you powerful because in a fight between a tiger and a lion, a fox always wins...' Raathi said as the room echoed with laughter.

"My aim is not to be powerful, but to be right. *Always,*" Ashwin said when the laughter subdued.

$\mathcal{J}$

"I don't care about being right or wrong, I just want to be powerful."

Somewhere in a small dark room, a man on a chair heard this for the third time. The man has just come to his senses; he felt like he has been asleep for decades. He wanted to get up from his place, but failed. He struggled for a few seconds and gave up; his legs were too weak. The brain was not transmitting orders properly; his head was aching badly. Even the soft rattling sound of the swing fan was unbearable. His eyes still could not adjust to the darkness. His throat was dry and he was sweating profusely. For him, this was hell. With every passing second, he wished for his death.

He did not know when his mouth finally croaked 'water'. There was no response to his demand, only the suffocating darkness. He waited and was engulfed by silence. He felt spiralling down; he needed water to pull him back and to show him hope. There wasn't any! He began losing it.

He thought he heard somebody speaking, 'I don't care about being right or wrong I just want to be powerful'. Was that his own conscience? For there was nobody around!

Will he finally die? Tears that trickled down his cheeks merged with the sweat on his neck!

He came to again when he felt a splash of water on his face. "More," he said shakily, and prepared himself for another splash, but that didn't happen. Instead he got a glass filled with it. He gulped it all at once. He imagined the hand that gave him the glass – a wheatish rugged man, with a bouncer-like appearance.

"Who are you and what do you want?" The man spoke rapidly groping in the dark. Water had restored some of his energy and it was time for negotiations.

"I can give you anything you want. Money? Name your price; you know I can give you a lot of it." He strained hard to see through the darkness. Nothing.

"Have you called my family yet?" the man continued. "Let me talk to them. I can ask them to transfer all the money from my private accounts in Switzerland." He waited for the reply but got none, so he continued, making the offer more attractive.

"And when I say money, I mean in the range of five hundred crores. Yes, five hundred crores or even more! Are you getting this? Just let me go." He sobbed then pulled himself up.

"I don't want to die! I am afraid to die. Save me please…"

The silence in the room was finally broken by the sound of a TV and the man prepared himself to meet his extortionist, but instead, Ashok Kumar Nandi heard the news of his own death.

He was alive for a reason, Nandi cried to himself. And the reason was not money, he thought and shuddered. He felt as if his heart would burst and he wailed like a woman. His consciousness began coming back. For the first time, he felt pain around his wrist as the nylon rope with which he was tied to the chair had cut his skin. Suddenly it dawned upon him that there was no darkness in the room. He had lost his sight.

♌

Sumona Thandi, Chairman and Managing Director of Thandi Group, was on her way to the airport. She looked at her watch when her car stopped at the first signal; it was ten to four. It would take at least an hour to get to the airport. Her flight was due at five! *Damn.*

Sumona Thandi had taken charge of all the major companies under Thandi Group soon after her father's sudden death ten years back. Under her leadership, the business had reached new heights, expanding vigorously in the Asia–Pacific region. Even though she was in a constant legal battle with her brother Prateek regarding unfair acquisition of wealth, she was undeterred. The business had grown threefold and that's what mattered!

Her tablet buzzed. It was an email from her executive assistant. The email was supposed to contain a business idea she would be proposing to the Department of Industrial Policy and Promotion (DIPP) later. A media file was attached. To her astonishment, it was a poorly recorded video of a dark room. Confused, she checked the details of the mail:

Sender: Vidyut Varma, her EA
Subject: 'DIPP Presentation for today'
Message: 'Final version post your feedback'
Time: 4:30 p.m.

She was about to close it, sure that Vidyut must have attached the wrong file, when a man appeared in the video.

The man was sitting on a chair. His face look pained, eyes sunken and distant, lips cracked, and hair dishevelled. But even in the dim light, the features were distinct and Sumona recognized that man instantly – Ashok Kumar Nandi! she gasped, closed the video, switched off her tablet and threw it on the car seat. She felt her driver stop momentarily. She was in shock. It wasn't the condition of the man that bothered her, it was the recording date at the bottom of the screen – yesterday's.

Ashok Kumar Nandi had died a week ago!

The car stopped at a signal and her driver turned his head to check if she was alright. She said she was. She wasn't. She was nervously rubbing her hands together, trying to keep her nerves calm. She has just seen a dead man alive. The car stopped again at another signal and the car TV screen rolled down.

"Rajesh! I am *okay*," she told the driver. "Thanks for the concern, but I don't want to be entertained, right now!"

The screen did not go up. It came to life. The same video began. Ashok Kumar Nandi started speaking in a hoarse voice. It looked like he had been crying a lot. His eyes looked distant and unfocussed.

"Sumona, you must be shocked to see me. Yes, I am alive. Honestly, right now, I don't want to be…"

"Rajesh! Switch off the damn video, for god's sake!" Sumona shouted, but the screen did not roll back. She noticed that the car had taken a random turn. It was speeding at 120 km/hr and the doors and windows were all locked. Any protest was useless.

"…we thought we are powerful, manipulators of the first order," Ashok Kumar Nandi was speaking in the video. "We were so involved controlling things that it never occurred to us that we could be manipulated too…. *Why not?* Look at me. I am supposed to be dead; killed in that helicopter crash. Rotor malfunction, they said. The police checked the death count. Nandi dead. File closed. News channels TRP high!" Nandi added angrily. "Police couldn't find out that I did not even board that flight. It was not that difficult. But they couldn't, because there weren't meant to."

He paused and took a deep breath to calm himself. "While we were always on top of our plans, we both made huge mistakes. You trusted the wrong people. I trusted you."

Sumona felt a knot in her stomach. Nandi continued talking about being trapped, but she wasn't listening. Her mind was racing; she had used Nandi for her benefits. From getting government support for her businesses, to changing her father's will, she had exploited Nandi's emotions for her. Pretending to love him, she made him do everything unethical which helped her to own one of the India's biggest business groups and become India's most powerful business woman.

After that Nandi was not required, as his position in the party was not commanding anymore; there were other people who could be used for the job, like Suresh Armugham. Besides, Armugham was not emotionally attached to her like Nandi; another reason why Nandi's elimination became inevitable. He had truly started loving Sumona and expected the same in return. It was not possible. She could not reject him outright; she could not tell him that she slept with him only because she wanted materialistic benefits in return. She could not tell him anything because he only had made her and hence could destroy her in the blink of an eye. Sumona had no choice but to wipe out Nandi, before he could *finish* her!

She contacted an aeronautic technician and compelled him to remotely interrupt rotor mechanism of the helicopter Nandi would use to fly from Delhi to Mumbai. The helicopter would lose navigation control followed by rotor malfunction, producing friction in the engine driveshaft, initiating a fire. Within a few seconds the gas in the engine would burst into flames and the helicopter would crash into the Thar. Everything was set. Everything went as planned, except that she never knew that Nandi had not boarded the flight.

Now, she was responsible for murdering four innocent people and somebody knew about it.

She looked up at the video again, when she heard the word 'demand'. Nandi was speaking.

"…Transfer all your assets and businesses to your brother."

What? My brother? Prateek?? Is he behind all this?

The car was now running on an expressway, away from the city. Following the instructions of the video, Sumona opened the envelope stuck under the passenger seat cover. She pulled out the green legal papers and checked the content.

It was an agreement to transfer the ownership of all the 120 companies that she owned to her brother Prateek. It was all in stringent legal lingo to ensure hassle-free transaction. She didn't even read the entire content and started signing it. While signing the last sheet, Sumona finally noticed the date of the agreement.

28 July 2013 – a month from that day.

♌

For a month, Sumona did not come to office or go to her house. Nobody had seen her, not even her mother. One could suspect foul play, especially after she abruptly cancelled her meeting with DIPP. She was responding to her emails, so Sumona Thandi was very much present virtually. She had even responded to some phone calls, but nobody knew where she was and why she was not meeting people.

"Acute depression," concerned friends and employees thought, "After all she was going through a lot."

"Good riddance," thought the others who hated her.

The family kept quiet; they had accepted her as she was - mercurial. During that period, she had spoken to her mother quite a few times. She just sounded tired.

Nothing unusual.

On the morning of the 28th of July, Sumona Thandi was found dead in her Colaba mansion. The subsequent autopsy report declared 'IV Pethidine overdose' as the prime cause of death.

That evening, over two billion USD were transferred from five different sources, to a bank account in Switzerland. Prateek was the sender; Hades the receiver.

♌

"She was a slut, with a vagina so big that it could take ten men at a time and would still have place for more. Her vagina was like her desires – endless!" Prateek said on the phone.

"I know she was my sister and all," he continued sipping his drink, "but she got the end she deserved. She thought I wouldn't know that she changed Daddy's will and removed my name from a hundred and twenty companies. Do you know, she along with Nandi, did everything possible to ensure that I was ripped off my sanity? As if the unfair distribution of Thandi Empire wasn't enough, she framed me in various scams and used her 'special' government connections to stop whatever businesses I owned. Moral-less! That is what she was, and now that she is gone, I don't want to be a part of any of her previous associations."

Ashwin's mouth felt dry when he heard this. Thandi group was a major funder for the Nationalistic Party under Sumona Thandi, and things seemed to be changing real fast now. There was apprehension in the party about the future flow of funds from Thandi group under the new management. Ashwin Jamwal had approached Prateek to continue the relationship between the Nationalistic Party and Thandi group. "Prateek ji," Ashwin began in his sweet cajoling voice, "there is no one who knows the importance of separating emotions from business better than you. What we are talking here is pure business. I am new to the post, so are you. Things are different from what they used to be."

Prateek laughed. "I like you. We should have drinks together sometime."

"Definitely."

"You are correct. I should separate emotions from business. You are smart, no doubt you are so popular. But tell me Mr Jamwal, how can I work with someone who has slept with my sister?"

"What?"

"Tell me something, how many times have you been inside my sister?"

Ashwin flushed with embarrassment, "Erm...none...never," he blurted.

"I believe you!" Prateek laughed. "My sister was into old perverts like Armugham, the ones who would do anything for a fresh pussy. Tell me, has he been inside my sister?"

"I don't know."

"And Raathi?"

"I really don't know."

Prateek let out a dry laugh. "The whole world knows!"

"Things have changed. I make decisions now."

"I know. Man, I like you! Let us meet for some drinks tomorrow."

Ashwin disconnected the call and looked at Raathi and Armugham. They had been listening to the conversation.

"You handled it pretty well," Raathi said smiling. To Ashwin's astonishment, neither Armugham nor Raathi look abashed.

"God, I hate so many things about politics," Ashwin shook his head.

Ashwin Jamwal

I never thought I would get into politics. I always wanted to get into the IAS. My distant uncle was an IAS officer working with the Ministry of Finance. I was awed by the respect he got. I wanted to be just like him.

Then I met Indra Mohan Raathi.

I first met him when I was in my second year of graduation. That day I was delivering a speech on behalf of the All India Students Association secretary Chandrabhan Yadav, to start a student movement on employment.

Under a big banyan tree located just outside Allahabad University, Arts Faculty, I was addressing a group of twenty odd students.

"Employment and employability are two different things," I said, "and our government has failed to give us both. Our government has opened up the economy and is boasting a GDP growth of 6%. But the employment which is supposed to be proportional to the growth grew by only 1.8%. I have serious doubts over the education policies and agenda of the planning commission because neither have they succeeded in penetration of primary and secondary education, nor have they been able to increase the GER in tertiary education." I paused as more people joined the crowd.

"If that was not enough, the competition for government services in India is becoming stiffer everyday and it's likely to get worse! You know why? Because students don't have choices! Vocational education is not promoted. An average graduate can only apply for government services which have limited seats, resulting in unemployment. Most of the students come here with aspirations to become IAS officers, but after years of hard work and failure, they begin appearing in all other examinations as well, only to be disappointed. It's not like they are not capable. They are. The thing is, there are way too many capable individuals, which makes all of them just average! Believe me, the government is indifferent; it's foolish to rely on them and wait for new policies. Nothing will ever happen. Status quo is comforting, status quo is profitable. Don't keep your hopes on the government or its young politicians! They don't know our miseries. Besides, these young leaders are chaperoned by old babool trees whose roots are deep in corruption. Nobody will bring in the change for you. You have to bring it yourself, I sincerely request all of you to sign up for your membership in the AISA and be a catalyst for change. The forms are available in the AISA office." I finished my speech with 'Jai Hind' and jumped off the makeshift wooden stage.

Arun Deb, my best friend, was waiting for me. He was smiling and frowning at the same time.

I patted his back. "So how was it?"

"I don't know. I didn't listen. Not interested!" He replied with irritation and started collecting some papers from the chair kept next to him.

"Did you study last night?" he asked me.

"World History, 17th century Renaissance, and then Chandu Bhaiya called—"

"And you stopped studying and began preparing for the education scenario."

I grinned.

"Tell me again...why are you doing this?"

"Because... "I began and was interrupted by a screeching sound from the loudspeaker. We turned and saw three gentlemen walking towards us. One of them looked familiar.

"Indra Mohan Raathi," said the familiar man, offering his hand.

"I know you!" I said as we shook hands, "You gave a speech on alternate education in India at a seminar in MONIRBA."

"I am impressed! You were there?"

"Yes, a friend had invited us. Your speech was the highlight of the programme for me."

"Thank you!" Raathi said smiling. "And today I heard you speak. Your speech was immaculate. For the first time somebody talked sense on that platform. What's your name, son?"

"Ashwin Jamwal," I said confidently.

"I see a great leader in you. Do you aspire to join mainstream politics?"

"Oh no, sir!" I said immediately. "What you saw today happened because I have my own frustration about Indian education. Yesterday Chandu Bhaiya asked me to deliver this speech because he himself was tied up somewhere else. I am preparing for UPSC and just like everyone else, I am also apprehensive about my future. My parents wanted me to study abroad, but I want to join the government services, because I want to do something for the country..." I stopped realizing that I had given a fairly long answer to a very direct question.

"Chandu? Chandrabhan Yadav? The All India Student Association secretary?"

I nodded.

"Good guy he is – Feisty! I just met him." I.M. Raathi spoke putting his arms around my shoulders.

"Ashwin, my son, when I talked about mainstream politics I did not mean the current parties. I meant my party, which would be different. Unlike all other parties, it would be people driven. It will have people like you who want to bring change to the country, people who are aggressive and sensible at the same time. You know what I am saying?"

I nodded silently. I was feeling so small in his presence.

Raathi removed his hand and told me about his aspirations to make a clean, corruption-free party which could change the entire political system of India.

"I don't know when it will happen," he said afterwards. "Five years or fifteen, or more. But it will happen, and when it does, we will have the best of the best in the party. And I want to mark you for that. What do you think?"

"Oh! Thank you sir," I said in embarrassment. "I am not sure of my future. I could be an IAS officer or a clerk. You never know, I could still be appearing in CSE after fifteen years. Good for me if I can consider politics as an option too."

"Don't make it an option," Raathi handed me a business card and left.

♋

Two years later I cracked CSE with a good rank. It was a happy time for us. My parents were on top of the world. My mother bragged, "Fifty-ninth rank all over India! And he is only twenty-three." My father hugged me like never before and said, "I knew you would do it!' I saw tears of pride in his eyes. That was the happiest moment of my life.

Jubilations doubled for us as Arun cleared the CSE the same year.

The evening before leaving for the academy, I met Arun by the MNIT railway tracks. We were celebrating with beers and tandoori chicken

"Now our parents can put a price tag on us – seventy-five lakhs on you, the IAS officer and fifty on me, an IPS," he said gulping his beer. "Whatever man, I am going to miss this."

"Miss what?" I asked. I hadn't been listening to him.

"This... this whole thing; running from the house, hiding here and drinking beer with you!" he said irritably.

I did not reply.

"What are you thinking?" Arun asked after a while.

"Nothing much!"

"Adya, eh?" Arun asked smiling. Adya Batra was my girlfriend of four years.

"Some random thoughts, not Adya."

I was thinking about the conversation I had had with I.M. Raathi two years ago when he first met me outside Arts faculty, and then later in the AISA office.

"If you want to change the system, be the system," Raathi told me when we met in AISA office. "It's a cliché, but it's true. By being an IAS officer, you can never significantly impact the governance of the entire nation. I have been an IAS officer and I know how it is. You won't be able to take a simple decision; someone or the other will always be unhappy. It's slavery of a different kind. We are mere puppets in the hands of ministers."

Being an IAS officer had been my only dream, but lately I was getting apprehensive.

♋

My first posting was in the small town of Dungarpur in Rajasthan. I wasn't happy with the place, but when I saw my room, I was filled with pride. Till this date, I remember that room; it was where, I thought it will all begin.

The room was quaint but clean and brightly lit. An old air conditioner on the top left side was making a loud whirling sound. There was a heavy mahogany table in the centre. On left of the table some files were neatly stacked next to a golden pen stand and a small Indian flag hoisted on the golden stand. On the right were few bizarre looking paper weights and a phone. The phone was covered with a red cloth for some reason.

I was excited to begin and after a quick exchange of pleasantries, I asked my deputy, Ravi Mundal, to stay back and fill me in.

"Congratulation sirji. Welcome to Dungarpur!" Ravi said taking his seat.

I picked up the first file labelled as 'Disputed religious property. Dt. 12th Sept. 1995. The file had not been cleared in five years. I asked Ravi about that file but instead he said:

"Dungarpur is a great place, sir. All the IAS officers have got very good postings from here. Our current cabinet secretary Pradhan ji also started his career here. This place is very lucky," he paused and dragged in some air through clenched teeth, much to my irritation.

"It's an old file, Mundal ji," I said quietly. "And it's the first on the stack. How difficult will it be to close it? Let us change a few things around here and ensure that all these files are cleared!"

"Of course sirji, we are here to help you. It's just that today is your first day and I wanted you to take it easy and not stress yourself over small matters," Mundal spoke politely.

"I will judge the triviality of the case," I said and opened the file. It was the cue for Mundal to leave.

It was a case of an acre of government land outside a small mosque which some students used for a protest. Nature and name of the protest was not disclosed, but apparently the student leader who started that protest turned out to be Hindu and the Imam of the mosque accused him of instigating communal rift in the society. Things became worse during the Muharram procession when the Hindu student leader was attacked. A communal riot followed which killed nine people. The property had been lying useless since then.

I could sense the political influence in this case. No action taken. Things remained buried in this file for five years.

First day!

I called Ravi again. He didn't look pleased to see the file in my hand.

"Sirji, it's your first day. Relax," he said, "Understand your work around here..."

"Understand my work?" I let out a fake cough. "I slogged for two years in the academy. I know my work!"

I wanted to act like a tough boy, but I must have done it poorly because this is what I got:

"Sirji, I have been posted here since 1991. I know how things work here. If since 1995 the file remained as it is, it will continue to remain so," he paused and sucked in some air. "Dungarpur as such is a quiet town. Enjoy your time here, make money and let these files be where they are. Why dig a forgotten grave and unnecessarily call for trouble? You are very young. Twenty-five or twenty-six? You are your parents' only child. Why worry your parents?"

"Is it a warning or a threat?" I said controlling my anger.

"Believe me, it's neither. I am just telling you how things work around here. Trouble will happen only when you work on the case. If I know the system any better, you will never get to work on it."

Ravi was correct. Exactly after ten days, I was transferred to Karauli, a nondescript district in Rajasthan. The reason was stated as 'official requirement'.

I left for Karauli in anger. So much for sleepless nights and all the hard work. So much for trying to close one file. During our training, closure of such files and quick decisions were applauded. In reality, its application had different ramifications. It is condemned and you are silently eliminated from the scene.

Karauli started on a similar note and met the same end. I was transferred again! I had four transfers in two years; my parents were getting worried. My mother would say, "Take leave and come home" after every transfer. I never went home. I was getting wary of continuous discussions on pragmatic morality and paradoxes of existence. I had started to accept things that I could not change – the IAS officers are mere puppets.

My fourth posting was in Nagaur. My mother spoke to me on my first day there; she was crying throughout the conversation. She knew my transfers were the results for doing right things and not following the system.

"For my sake, please stay low. You cannot do a thing in this corrupt system. Don't try to change it. Please, beta."

I understood; I couldn't move a pebble in this system. I was getting tired of the whole bloody cycle! I didn't want to go through the endearing process of achieving nothing, again.

So for the next six months, I did not try to change the system. Old files remained on the table and controversial issues were avoided. For six months, I went to office at nine and left at six sharp!

But then there was no contentment. I started losing my confidence. The slugfest of right and wrong has been going on since eternity, the facts had been twisted so many times that the sides had switched silently, or so it seemed. I wasn't sure what was right or wrong anymore.

I remember having a mild headache that day after the office. Kisanji, my cook, put a cup of tea on the table the moment I slumped on the sofa.

"Will you have non-veg today, sir?" he asked politely

"Anything." I noticed he did not leave so I added, "I can have non-veg."

I always feel that these so called illiterate domestic helps are much more sincere towards their jobs than the qualified officers sitting in government offices and drawing hefty salaries for doing nothing.

"You look unwell," he said.

"A slight headache."

"Should I give you a massage?" he asked with concern

"I will be okay," I said drinking my tea.

"Please go out today," Kisanji said empathically. "See the city. I have asked driver Bhuvan to stay back. He will take you around. You have not gone out at all!"

Kisanji was right; I hadn't gone out ever since I had come to Nagaur! I needed to get out just to pull myself from the abysmal feeling of self-contempt. So I left. I didn't take the vehicle though. I wanted to walk.

After walking on the clean pavement adjoining government bungalows, I took a random left to a narrower road. That road was a complete contrast to the wider one connecting it. It was cramped, dirty and noisy, but it was full of life. The smell of masala wafting from various kitchens reminded me of Allahabad and I kept walking till I saw an SUV that had blocked the road in such a way that even pedestrians were struggling to pass through. I realized I could not move further, so I decided to turn back, only to find myself stuck in another chaos. A truck which was unloading gravel in front of one of the houses had left only bare minimal space for other vehicles to pass. Even that had been blocked, thanks to an impatient tempo driver, who miscalculated the width of his vehicle and got stuck in that space, making it impossible for the pedestrians to pass!

I was looking for other exits. Frustrated, I felt my pockets and realized I had forgotten to bring my phone. I started regretting my decision. Only half an hour back I was feeling happy to be out of the house and now I just wanted to go back!

I stopped an elderly man on a scooter and asked for directions. He said he would drop me at the main road and from there I could take an auto to reach my destination.

When I sat on that scooter, I didn't know that it would change my life forever

"Nagaur has changed a lot," the old man said as we started to move. Soon he began ranting about the district administration and how it had deteriorated. I let him speak as he wasn't lying.

"MNCs have opened up," that man continued. "Girls wearing western clothes are going around with boys on streets. It used to be a conservative place, not like Jaipur; but now it has changed. There is no problem with development. It's just that development in India is superficial. I talk about this to the current generation and they mock me. They point at the number of cars, ATMs, banks and plush shops while I talk about the depleting condition of the roads.

The man turned his scooter into another dim lit alley. The only light illuminating the entire alley was one coming from the porch lights of a big house. As the scooter passed that house, the old man shook his head. "This house belongs to some politician. Not even a big politician, but a small one, very small in fact. But this politician will have more money in this house than an average Indian can ever earn in his lifetime. The common man in India is subjugated by both upper and lower grades. The entire system of India is faulty. Common men like me are programmed to stay indoors in fear, never to speak up, neglected throughout. What do you say?"

"Hmm."

The old man fell quiet and then spoke, "You must be wondering why this senile man is babbling?"

"No, uncle, in fact I am —"

The old man did not let me finish, "Even my Missus says that I have become senile. But what to do? With every passing year we hope for betterment in the country. Better governance, better facilities, better treatment of the common man. But every year the common man is disappointed. Is it so hard to find a good leader in a country of billion? Apparently it is. You know why? Because either Indian people are too honest or too corrupt. Either they are sadhus or shaitans. For a perfect government you need a hybrid of both. India needs someone who is righteous enough to ethically utilize the taxpayer's money and conniving enough to straighten up other corrupt people. We need an honest man with a gun to run this country. Sadly we don't have anyone who is up for this."

He dropped me and even helped me get an auto. He apologized for his rant and I was thankful to him for taking me out from that madness.

When I went to bed that day, I was tired and frustrated. The events of the evening had not turned out as planned. They started on a good note but ended up miserably. I was still depressed and helpless. As the darkness engulfed me, I started hearing random voices in my head; from hoarse voice of the current CDO, to exhilarating shrieks of children from the alley; from an irritating ringtone, to my mother's voice. I don't know when I succeeded in silencing those voices to hear my own conscience. Strangely, it repeated what that old man has said:

"We need an honest man with a gun..."

I sat up. Why hadn't it occured to me earlier? As a supporter of AISA and as the head boy in school, I had exposed the malicious activities in my alma mater. I was an honest person adopting dishonest means to do right things. If I could do it then, I could do it now.

No, I wasn't trying to emulate a Bollywood hero! I really wanted to make things right. Besides, I did not want to give up; not without trying. If I succeed, there would be nothing like it. If I failed? I did not think of it. Death perhaps?

From the next day onwards, I dedicated all my energies to develop a foundation for my new modus operandi. While inside the walls of the government office, I would continue my mundane routine in Nagaur; outside, I would be working to straighten up the system. So I made a thorough dossier on each officer and politician related to my function. I also made a close network of informants who could provide me reports of coveted activities happening behind my back. I was determined to tackle the system in its own way.

Finally after four months, I got a chance to test the effectiveness of my informants and my newly adopted avatar of the 'honest man with a gun'. This happened when one of the informants tipped me about a scam on a construction tender for government schools in villages of Naguar, under RTE. What appalled me was that the name of the company to get the tender was decided even before the tender notice was made public. I had always thought that companies bribe government officers after applying for jobs and tenders; I didn't know that it happens much before the announcement! There was lot of corruption in the system, and it needed cleansing. I must say it was quite amusing to see the performances of the Chief Development Officers and Sub District Magistrate. Sitting across my table, they were actually debating to ensure that the best quotation for the tender is proposed, as if they were really worried about the tax payers' money; as if they didn't already know the name of the company which will get the tender – 'Subra Infrastructure Pvt. Ltd'.

For a moment I thought of rejecting their suggestion just to bum them off, but I didn't.

Instead I said, "Where do I sign?"

They both looked happy on successfully completing the task, silently patting each other's back for conveniently fooling a DC. It made me wonder how many DCs were being fooled by such corrupt officers every day? How many times have I signed such papers relying on deliberations of these so called adept and experienced government employees? Well, things were about to change. I fixed an appointment to meet the Mayor of the city later that day.

When Mayor Rangbahadur Singh saw me, he smiled; his smile more acerbic than cordial.

"So how are you today, Jamwal Sahib?" Singh leaned back on his chair. He used to call me *naya bachcha*, the new kid. He briefly glanced at the blue file, which I had kept on his desk before sitting, and asked, "What is this file?"

"Papers for government school construction tenders," I replied. "The tender has gone to Subra Infrastructure."

"Okay," he said with complete indifference. Only with years of practice comes the ability to maintain a straight face in such situations. There was no sign of recollection of the company's name on the Mayor's face.

"I feel it's a good one, Singh Sahib," I said opening my laptop.

"Good, good! You have adjusted here. Tea?"

"I had some before coming here," I said quietly clicking on one of the files in my laptop. "The CDO and SDM convinced me after an hour of debate that Subra should get the tender."

The Mayor shrugged and smiled convivially, "Is there anything you want from me, Jamwal Sahib?"

"Yes. I want you to stop the contract!"

"What?" Rangbahadur Singh sat up. "You are telling me to stop the contract? What do I have to do in this? If you don't like it, don't sign it!" he added angrily.

"I am telling you nothing," I said smiling and turning the laptop screen towards him. "I have come here for some ceremonial discussion, now it's up to you to stop it, for reasons I don't know. As for me, I have signed the document in front of the SDM and CDO," I said before playing the video.

Singh sat in shock as he watched himself taking money from owners of Subra infrastructures while a woman in a short shimmering dress licked his cheeks.

After a week, Subra withdrew its application. That was my first success; it gave me confidence to implement such methods for carrying out government functions rightfully.

I remain posted in Nagaur for three years – my longest tenure in an office. I operated righteously there and nobody interfered. In fact, corrupt officers began cooperating. I was able to bring significant change in the district. Local dailies praised my administration and my acclaim reached the whole of Rajasthan. So when I was transferred to Udaipur, I was more confident and better equipped.

I remember waking up to the cold sensation of water that day. The cook was kneeling next to my bed with a wet cloth, and the driver and gardener were standing near the door. They looked concerned. The cook helped me get up. As I sat up, I felt an excruciating pain in my head and an urge to throw up.

What happened?

"Here, have some water. The cook gave me a glass and watched me drink. "How are you feeling, now?"

I looked at him, confused, and did not reply. What happened?

The cook touched my forehead and spoke, "You don't have fever, but something is terribly wrong. You have been sleeping since Tuesday."

He made me lie back again. "Somebody must have cast an evil eye on you! I will remove it and I will call the doctor."

"Tuesday?" I asked weakly."

"It is Thursday today, sir. You've slept for forty-four hours."

"Forty-four hours?" I repeated absently"

"You came home late on Tuesday and...umm..." the cook hesitated, looking for better word then said "You were... umm...very drunk..."

"Drunk?" Inebriated?

"Sir, Raman got you inside. You were so drunk that you couldn't walk. We put you in bed."

"Raman," I looked at the driver, "Where... did I get drunk?"

"Lohia ji's bungalow!" Raman replied

"I will bring some coffee for you," the cook said and left.

Raman continued, "You went there around half past four and came out at ten supported by Lohia's men. You were smelling badly of alcohol. You vomited in the car twice and were talking about some rally."

I remember going to Lohia's residence on account of a rally. Srujan Singh Lohia was the state secretary of the Opposition party. He was known for vandalising properties in the name of student agitations and he was planning to steer another student movement on Friday with an aim to destroy shops in Shakti Nagar. I got to know that an affluent businessman in Udaipur had paid him a hefty amount to carry out this job. I didn't know whether students were aware of Srujan Singh's true intentions; whether they had got a cut from the profit or not; but I thought it was unfair to punish students for those crimes and not Srujan Singh Lohia, the actual criminal. I had to stop that nonsense.

"Leaking information of one connection to another is a serious breach of trust and that's not what good friends do," I told Lohia quietly. I was alone with him in his study and he was absolutely quiet.

"Yes, I know you work for both the opposition and the ruling party," I added.

Lohia stared at me menacingly and spoke just above the whisper, "I can get you killed here and nobody will know."

"Of course you can. Yet, you won't," I paused and corrected myself. "You can't. In fact, you must not, if you are an intelligent man."

That was when I first felt a sudden pain along the cervical vertebrae, which I ignored.

"If the rally happens, irrespective of whether I live or not, your facts will surface and reach the right people," I continued with more confidence. "You know the consequences of the same, don't you?"

Lohia stared at me so I leaned forward and said, "Of course you do. They will kill you and nobody will know a thing."

I felt the pain rising up, but let the feeling go. I would be done with him in five minutes anyway.

"And don't make me do things I don't want to do," I continued. "If I die, besides your double crossing activities, the Sanganer case may also open up. I am sure you wouldn't want that."

Lohia gaped. I had mentioned the most infamous scandal from his past. The rape and murder of five foreign tourists; two of them minors.

"I leave you now with a choice, Lohia ji," I said getting up. "I trust you to make the right decision."

I began to leave, but felt dizzy. I remember holding the chair for support, and then no recollection of what happened afterwards.

I sighed, relieved to know that I wasn't given anything by Srujan Lohia, because I fainted at his residence. But suddenly I felt anxious that even though I may not have had alcohol, something was given to me. I quickly checked for injection marks; there weren't any. The cook came back with a cup of coffee, and then it dawned on me. Earlier that day, I had taken coffee instead of tea. Coffee is a great drink to put a drug in, as it eliminates the smell of the drug without effecting its chemical properties. Damn!

I started to have a bad feeling about it! I picked up my phone and saw thirty missed calls, a majority of them from an informant Suraj. I called him.

"Where have you been, sir?" he asked, clearly anxious.

"What's the bad news?" I asked instead.

"Don't you know already?"

"I know nothing!" I said empathically. "I had been drugged. I was unconscious for forty four-hours...since Tuesday!"

There was silence at the other end. Suraj then spoke softly. "That means you did not go to Lohia's residence?"

"I did! And I fainted there. I woke up only a few minutes back."

"That means..." Suraj spoke.

"Means what?"

"You did not plan to instigate a communal riot?"

"What the fuck!"

"Sir, Lohia will be reaching the TBN channel office with a video in which you are talking about a student rally that will turn into a communal riot of a scale Udaipur has never witnessed," Suraj paused before speaking again. "You have used pretty nasty words against the Muslim community. You have cursed Islam, saying that this is your vengeance against a revenue officer who had made your life hell when you were training under him."

"Shaukat sir?" I said trying to remember the name of the officer. "I do not hate him!"

Suraj sighed and continued. "I have seen that video. Not only you justified your reasons for starting a communal riot, you even demanded three crores from Lohia to protect his properties. Lohia will reach TBN tomorrow. The student rally is tomorrow. I have heard he will tell the press that he cannot let something like this happen for his profit. A person of your disposition should be exposed. Hello sir? Are you listening?"

"I am.... I am."

I was in shock. There was a video of me planning to instigate a communal riot because Shaukat sir troubled me years ago. That was ridiculous! I have no grudges against Shaukat Ali. He was just another officer who trained me. I definitely do not hate Islam as I have been visiting the Ajmer Sharif Dargah every month for the last three years! Yet there was a video stating otherwise. AVs are accepted as evidence of crime.

There are drugs which can align the thinking process in a particular manner. Above all, the AV can be tampered too. I could be answering questions, which were then mixed accordingly to make an evidence video. It was very much possible.

"Sir? Sir?" Suraj was calling out.

"I didn't do it!" I said exasperatedly. "There are drugs! There are ways to tamper audio visuals."

"I know! I thought about it too, sir. There are drugs which could make you say things inducted in your brain. There is no need for AV tampering then."

"In that case I cannot prove my innocence, even after frame by frame examination of the tape..." I was talking more to myself now, trying to figure a way out of this mess Lohia had put me in.

"No, I don't think so!"

"Traces of the compound might be present in my blood..."

"I doubt it. It happened two days ago. By now, the compound must have been broken into its primary elements."

"Should I go to TBN?" I asked.

There was silence for a while, and then Suraj let out a sigh and spoke. "Sir, the media in India is the worst of its kind. It doesn't have a conscience; it favours only the ones with mullah. It's dirty. Don't do that!"

"Then what should I do?" I asked dejected. "So that's it? That's how I will go? With a tainted record? Is there no way out?'

"There is." Suraj said calmly, "You resign today."

"What?"

"Resign, sir! That's your only option to save yourself. Say health reasons, better opportunities in the private sector, political aspirations... anything! But just get out of this shit. If I know your enemies any better, they will transfer three crores in your account before going to the press and then you will be stuck."

"But...how..."

"Sir, please understand. Everything, fucking everything is planted! It is one multilevel, highly networked plan of a very smart individual. You have been manipulated so that you can remove yourself from the system."

"They could have had me killed."

"Earlier maybe, not now. There have been way too many IAS deaths in the past year. The government is acting swiftly to nail down the culprits and punish them due to the tremendous public pressure. Why would anyone eliminate you, when you can be removed?"

I covered my face. Darkness was comforting. While I thought I had found a way to deal with the debauchery in the system, I was being manipulated. I felt swirling down

I had refused to be a puppet. I had tried changing the system. And I had failed. The entire system is rotten and everybody is being manipulated by somebody more powerful.

In less than twenty-four hours evidence against me will be given to the media, and I will be accused of committing a crime which can ruin my life forever, I thought. There was nothing I could do to stop it, so I got up from my bed, opened my laptop and typed my resignation.

Then I went home. Ten days later, I met my mother and told her my plans about joining a political party.

"What?" she asked without even looking at me. She was sorting and folding the washed clothes on my bed.

My mother is a humble woman; a retired English Professor and a housewife. She is one of those women who could quote likes of Kafka in academic gatherings and cook a perfect mutton curry at home.

"I am joining a party!" I repeated, louder this time

"Don't be stupid, Ashu!" She retorted and turned to face me. I was sitting on a pouf near the dresser. I had not shaved and looked messy. My mother hated such negligence towards personal grooming. Under normal circumstances, she would have asked me to shave that very moment; but that day, she just kept quiet.

"Politics is not easy," she said softly, "I think you should go for MBA. Your father and I were talking last night. Finish your MBA from some international college and —"

"Please, Ma. We have had this discussion," I said a little agitated at her outright rejection. "You know I went for the civil services because I wanted to do something for the country—"

"We have listened to you! I have listened to you," she interjected. "You always had your way, starting from opting for Maths instead of computers in the 12th standard. You got 89% only because of Maths; Arun got 93 because he opted for computers. Or taking History during graduation even though your mother was an English professor in the university. And you almost flunked in History!"

"What? You are starting from my 12th standard results? Unbelievable!"

"I am not done yet!" she continued angrily. "Then you became an IAS officer! And not just any Deputy Collector, but an honest Deputy Collector," she added sarcastically.

"Ma, you only told me to be honest."

"Being honest is not wrong, son! But imposing morality on others is. They will not learn! You don't want bribes, you don't take them... but you can't ask somebody else to follow you. If that person knew anything about morality, he wouldn't have taken the money in the first place."

"I am so upset, Ma!"

"Beta please understand," she began softly. "Now when I started telling myself that you will pursue a safer career, you are coming to me with another caprice – I want to join politics! It's called politics for a reason and you are not meant for it. Corruption starts there! Honest people do not last in the political arena; they are either forced to join the masses or are eliminated. I know you, nothing can force you to do something unethical and what if—" she choked as tears welled up her eyes.

I gently made her sit on the bed and put my head on her lap. I started speaking softly,

"I understand, Ma, but I request you to listen to me too. I wish I could tell you what I have gone through. Reality is not what it looks like on paper. I thought if I could manage things as the DC, macro level operations would not be difficult. I tried everything from being submissive to aggressive, being a sycophant, a manipulator, a strategist, and even a spy." I smiled briefly and continued, "But what I couldn't be was corrupt. The entire system is immoral. The processes are all flawed and designed to favour the majority. And unfortunately, corrupt officials make the majority! I realized that the system needed cleansing, but nobody was up for it. I tried and I tried hard, but failed, because IAS officers are mere puppets, Ma, nothing else."

"And through politics you think you can clean the system, eh?" she said stroking my hair gently.

"It all starts with politics. Ministers have all the power."

She smiled. "You are talking like a kid."

"I am not joining an ordinary party," I said getting up, "but one which has many people like me. It's a fairly new party called Nationalistic Party. It is formed by a man named I.M. Raathi, with an aim to bring change in the country. It's a clean corruption-free party..."

"Nationalistic Party?" my mother squinted.

"Yes! I met the founder almost ten years back, and if it gives you any confidence, Mr Raathi said that I have all the skills to be a Prime Minister."

I had to stop there as my mother started laughing uncontrollably.

I spoke again, when she had stopped giggling.

"Laugh all you want. He said that to me ten years back! He met me a few more times in Rajasthan, for official reasons, of course, and has always encouraged me to join his party. After I resigned, I had two options: either I give up and study in INSEAD business school with Puja Maasi's son; or I could continue working towards the betterment of my country. I opted for the latter because I didn't want to give up. Besides, the party has enough funds, they are ready to give me a 30% hike on my current salary. Of course there'll be no perks, but who needs perks?"

"We have never imposed our decisions on you, but politics is called politics for a reason, beta I do not want to see you disappointed," she said getting up.

"Just give me two years. If I can't manage, I will go abroad, study and work, mint money and buy Mercedes and go..."

"I got it!" she said laughing. "You have made up your mind, but I want you to break it to your father."

I wrapped my arms around her. "You tell Papa, please!" She shook her head

"Also tell Adya! She should know."

"That I will do, but you have to handle Papa."

I met Adya in the evening and told her about my plans and aspirations. She was pursuing her career in journalism and had travelled from Delhi to meet me. She was not happy with my decision either, so to cheer her up I added, "Do you know many CMs ask IAS officers to touch their feet?"

"What? It doesn't make sense," Adya said irritably.

"I am telling you about the advantages of joining politics!" I said pleasantly.

"You are not serious," she said irritated.

"What's wrong in joining a party? I will be earning just as much."

"What's wrong with an MBA?"

"I will end up miserable in a nine to five job. You know that!"

"I also know you are way too honest for politics," Adya said moving her shoulders to ward off the exhaustion. "What about our marriage? We were supposed to get married this year."

"That we will," I said gently massaging her shoulders.

"You have to be settled, Ashwin!" Adya said after a while. "Dad will never approve of a party worker. An orange-clad neta. You understand that, right?"

"I won't be the PM tomorrow." I frowned.

"That's what, Ashwin!" Adya said turning to face me. "It hardly matters to me if you join politics, engage in guerrilla warfare, or start a coup, but Dad?"

"I will take some time to settle down. Will you wait?" I asked her finally.

"I will," she said and nodded.

I met Adya's father after a few days. He wasn't displeased at my decision; he was furious.

"You want us to wait?" he barked.

"Only for a couple of years," I said gathering all my strength to speak.

"And what guarantee do I have that you will not quit the party and ask for a couple of years again? You postponed the marriage last year as well. I am a father and I cannot marry my daughter to a fickle minded man."

"I for one have a very focused mind," I replied in frustration. "My agenda has always been clear; I want to be instrumental in the development of the country. I want to clean the system. I may be taking a different approach, but my life goals are fixed—"

"And I don't see Adya in your life goals!"

"Adya is there!" I emphasized.

"No Ashu! She doesn't fit anywhere. She is like a puzzle piece that you thought would complete your life's picture. And in an attempt to finish the picture, you are forcibly inserting that piece. You are hammering it, twisting it. But you know what, the piece won't fit, because it never was part of that puzzle."

"Uncle, I love Adya!" I spoke finally, after I couldn't come up with an analogy to match his.

"No Ashu. She loves you! Her love is unconditional. Even today she is ready to give up her dream job and start a life with you. Can you do the same? Can you give up on your aspirations and marry her?"

I wasn't ready for this! I stammered, "I...umm...err..."

Anant Batra raised his hand, "I got my answer Ashu!"

Deciding to tackle Anant Batra when he would be less furious, I busied myself in the party activities.

I came back to Allahabad after six months, to overlook operations of the first party office in the city. I pressed the door bell numerous times to wake up my parents early in the morning. I turned to look at Adya's house, which was just across the street, and saw a lock. It was not like I have never seen that house locked, but for the first time, my heart sank.

I asked my mother about them and she said they had left Allahabad

"Left?" I asked her again, "Forever?"

"Yes!"

"Where are they?"

"Alberta!"

"Canada?" I said looking at the rim of my cup. Adya had not told me anything when she spoke to me last week.

"Did they give a phone number or anything?" I asked feeling anxious.

My father left abruptly to show his displeasure.

"No! They didn't even wish us goodbye." My mother sighed.

"Did Adya leave me anything?" I asked desperately.

I was trying to find the last straw, with which I could cling and sail.

My mother shook her head.

I called Arun to inquire about Adya and got nothing. For years, I had ignored Adya's secret pleas for togetherness. And from that day, there wouldn't be any.

With Adya gone, I immersed myself into party activities. My contributions in the Rajasthan second state assembly elections were humongous. My campaigns for the general election could not be overlooked as well. I was getting popular among the young party members. I was becoming an icon of sorts for the Indian youth.

Just seven years in the party and I had already become its president and a strong PM candidate.

Yes, I know I didn't want to be in politics; yes I know I had lost Adya for this. Was that worth it? I don't know. But I have realised that there is something attached to the power of politics that is addictive. Power to influence, power to make yourself heard, power to make you important; the same power which could give even useless and corrupt politicians like Nandi a three-day coverage on national media.

2

Somewhere near the small town of Chengalpettu, a bunch of villagers took their bovines for a weekly bath. The only water for this purpose was in a pool behind a Karthkiyen Temple. Earlier this pool was used for ablution, before visiting the temple. The pond is no longer sacred and was majorly used for dumping temple waste.

Viswa removed some more polythene covers, biscuit wrappers and withered hibiscus flowers, to dip the used paint bucket deep for clean water. It was very common to find strange objects in that pond like spare cycle parts, scary dolls with no arms, awkwardly shaped iron pieces, so on and so forth, but what came out today made Viswa shiver.

"Ennachu?" the other villagers gathered around him, while he stood still in shock. He was looking at something that has just fallen from his bucket on the back of his buffalo

The skeleton of a human hand.

Villagers searched the entire pond but couldn't find the other parts of the body. The hand was then turned to the nearest police station.

Station in charge, Venkatesh R. looked at that hand in the small box. The skin was still attached to some of the fingers. Venkatesh shuddered at the thought of the increasing barbaric instincts in humans. The hand had been cut with a strong blow, just below the carpals. He usually sat on a case for some time before sending it to the regional headquarters in Chennai, but not that day. He didn't want to investigate another case of woman slaughter.

"Isn't it strange? We have so many cases of female foeticide in India. They are not allowed to be born. And if we let them live, they are raped, tortured for dowry and killed," he paused and looked at the woman constable uncomfortably. "And then you start thinking, female foeticide is not wrong. Why let them live and give them hope when they are destined to—"

His voice trailed off. "I have two daughters. God knows what the future holds for them."

The regional police headquarter at Chennai received the hand, and the officer there had the same thoughts as Venkatesh: 'another woman died in suffering'. Forensics extracted the DNA from that hand and ran it through the existing database of the missing and defunct list from Chennai. No match found. They then expanded their database to the entire southern region and got the same result. Though it was kind of preposterous, but the forensics ran the test on the national database. It took two weeks for the computer to finally yield the result.

♌

Deputy Commissioner Loganathan rubbed his eyes and looked at the report again.

"How is that even possible?" he asked.

"That's the result the machine gave us," the young forensic intern shrugged awkwardly.

Loganathan nodded. The results were astonishing. He called the CBI immediately.

The DNA matched with that of a man who had died three months ago, nearly two thousand kilometres away in a helicopter crash.

Ashok Kumar Nandi.

♌

Hades established connection with Prateek.

"They found a piece of Nandi's body in Tamil Nadu," Prateek said nervously. "I don't want to know what you did to him, but if the case reopens —"

"They will never reopen the case,'" Hades interrupted.

"What? You took care of it?" Prateek asked in relief.

"No. I didn't take care of it. But I know nobody wants to scrutinize the death of a corrupt politician. Too many names are there to be blamed and too much risk associated with it."

"What....? How can you be so sure?"

"I have been in this shit long enough to know how things work. Nothing will happen."

"Who are you?"

"It's immaterial. Your job is done, I got my price. Knowing my identity is not required."

Hades couldn't sleep. He sat up and lit a cigarette to stop the cacophony of the Arabic and English playing in his head. He was facilitating an illicit energy deal. While he chose to moderate the meeting on the phone, his most trusted men were physically available to resolve immediate issues. The deal was supposed to close that day. It didn't happen. The meeting started on a positive note but soon the discussion went awry, dominated by verbal spats and abuses. Hades had never imagined that the most aristocratic politicians and influencers of the world could behave so, but then instincts are all the same. Emotions do not discriminate. There will be fights for a piece of land, for food, for power. Quantity differs, instincts remain the same. Intrinsic, ingrained.

His subordinates succumbed to the pressure of higher officials. They were equally shocked to see their darker sides, but only in such moments your tenacity is tested. They kept mute and he regretted not joining the meeting in Addis Ababa.

"Incompetent bastards!" He threw his cigarette in disgust. He felt he was getting farther from his goal – *to become the most powerful person in the world.* His quest to seek power was deep-rooted, its origin unknown.

He had faded memories of his past which flashed in his sleep. Nightmares. Strangely, the faces from the past had faded, places blurred, but the pain remained as it is; the pain of being the smallest, most insignificant person in the world; the pain of being pushed around, being manipulated.

The pain of being the right one.

He looked outside the window. His mind wandered and took him to Chennai Marina Beach. He had been there a few days back. Walking barefoot on the sandy beach, admiring the vastness of the Bay of Bengal, he stumbled upon something hard. He dug it out. It was a perfectly good toy gun. He was about to throw it back, when he saw a small boy looking at it. *One man's trash is another man's treasure.* The boy hesitated, intimidated by the presence of a stranger and stood still. Hades offered the gun to him. The boy took it, grinned and left.

All of a sudden Hades felt uneasy. There was something familiar about that grin, the hesitation, the whole environment. Déjà vu.

A memory came to life

He must have been five years old then, the same age as the little boy whose grin brought the memory back. He was sitting on a torn polythene sheet blowing air into the balloons. The memory was so vivid that he could feel the warmth of the sand on his legs. A one year boy was sitting next to him, on the torn jute sack. They both were only a few feet away from a balloon shooting stall – an arrangement rather, balloons were stuck between two threads, tied across a wooden scaffold.

He wasn't looking up as if he was ashamed of himself. Avoiding eye contact with the people, he was keeping the bloated balloons in a big yellow polythene. Occasionally the little boy would crawl up to him to play with the balloons, but he would push him away.

There was a woman standing near the stall. She was wearing a bright orange sari, draped shabbily around her waist. Her long hair was braided and had a shrivelled string of jasmine. She was arguing with four boys who had come to her stall. A shooter gets ten pellets for two rupees per chance. She argued that all the four boys had had two chances each. The boys disagreed.

"I am sure all four of you have played twice so that's sixteen rupees," she said holding the four rupees in her hand. The boys refused to take it.

"Two of us shared! That makes it fourteen!" a boy replied coming forward. "Don't cheat us!"

"The whole beach knows Vijaya!" she said getting conscious of the people gathering around them. "Vijaya never cheats!"

"I don't care. Today you are cheating," said one of the boys, angrily. "Give us our money or we will call the police."

None of the spectators interfered, they all just stood there..

The woman gathered herself, feeling small in the presence of so many people. Her face softened and eyes welled up. She took out another two rupees and gave it to the boy.

"At least give me one rupee, we will eat today," she added softly.

"Why? What will you do with all the money you have just got?" The boy spoke sarcastically.

The other boys laughed and the crowd began dispersing.

"Take this," said one of the boys as he gave her twenty-five paise before leaving.

The woman put the coin in her blouse and tucked the rest of the money under the sheet.

"Blow fast!" she instructed him.

He remembered blowing more balloons, continuous clanking of the gun, more people coming in, a few more fights, and then it was dark. Night had fallen and the beach was quiet. He saw himself packing the guns and pellets in a torn sack. The small boy was sleeping. The woman was squatting next to him counting the earnings of the day. Before she could finish, some men approached; mechanically, she handed them some money. A man with long teeth counted and returned five rupees.

"It looks torn, change it," she did and resumed counting. Soon a man in police uniform approached her.

"Vijayaamma! You had quite a good day today!" he said grinning.

"Ille sir, just regular," she said getting up.

"Don't fool me, Vijaya. I saw that you gave extra five to Kadir anna's people. You give money to goons, but what about the people who are protecting you from them?"

The woman shot him a glance.

"I deserve to get an extra five today!" he said moving his head sideways, "Or else I will tell your husband about the stuff you have there," he added looking straight at her cleavage. The woman covered it immediately. She was worried about the money she had tucked in her blouse, not her dignity.

"If I will give you five extra, my earnings of the day will come to just 21," she cried. "What will we eat? Have mercy!"

"My children need to be fed too, Vijayamma!" the policeman added empathetically. "You know it's illegal to put up a stall on this part of the beach? I gave you permission to do so, so you can earn more money, but you never give it a consideration." He looked around to ensure that nobody was listening to their conversation and continued, "There are other ways in which you can pay me, though," he added touching her shoulders. She immediately gave him the money and left hurriedly, the small boy clinging on her waist.

Hades saw himself following her, dragging the oversized sack. He fell numerous times before reaching a dingy room. The woman was squatting near a kerosene stove boiling something in an aluminium vessel. A drunken man was sitting next to her, looking helplessly at the money in his hands.

"I need some money for rice," the woman spoke softly. "We have not eaten anything since morning."

The man stood up groggily and kicked her. She fell inches away from the stove.

"You want rice for twenty rupees? This is all you earned?" The man spoke angrily. "I slog all day and you give me this!"

"At least I give you something!" the woman shouted getting up. "You spend all the money on alcohol."

Her reply made the man furious. He pulled her by her hair; her shrivelled jasmine fell on the ground and she shrieked in pain. The man, indifferent to her pain, started hitting her with his slippers. The small boy began howling. The noise attracted the neighbours.

Nobody interfered. They all just stood there and watched.

"I will say it again. You are a drunkard and incompetent," the woman shouted.

"And you are competent?" The man gripped her neck and added sarcastically "You don't even have the looks to sell!"

The woman's eyes widened; so much for keeping her dignity intact. The man loosened his grip and she began coughing violently. He looked at her in disgust and started to go out of the room when he heard the distinct sound of coins falling on the floor. Surprised, he turned and saw the woman leaning over a few coins, which had fallen from her clothes.

"Leave these!" she said waving frantically around her as the man tried to pick up the fallen money. "I beg you! It's for our food."

"Bitch! Liar," the man started hitting her trying to get past her. She did not budge. He turned to her like a mad animal. Lifting her with all his strength, he kicked her hard. She stumbled and fell.

This time over the kerosene stove.

The aluminium vessel rolled down the slanted floor.

Hades saw the crowd rush inside, brushing past him. He stood there clutching the big sack, looking at the woman's body catching fire in the blink of an eye.

"Amma!" he began crying. He felt an arm around his shoulders that prevented him from going inside.

Back in the present, Hades was hyperventilating. Amma? Amma? His heart began beating faster and he felt warm. He would feel pain after every flashback, but not to this intensity. He knew exactly why the pain had aggravated.

In all his other memories, he saw himself and only himself trying to fight it out. But for the first time, he had seen his family – *his mother*. The subjugation must have been a regular thing for her because she conceded to everyone. This is how it works. After a while, you become accustomed to suppression.

Hades sat on the edge of his bed, still shivering from that memory. It happened again – the same plebeian feeling. He didn't want to get inured to the subservience. He wanted control.

Only if he would have been a little powerful back then, he would have killed the policeman, the goon *and his father.* He drank some water and tried to remember what had happened afterwards. Had his mother survived? What about that kid? And his father? He closed his eyes and thought hard, but nothing came back to him.

Indra Mohan Raathi was composed before the interview. The interviewer, he observed, looked jittery – shouting orders, flipping pages, validating reports, talking on phone and typing at the same time. This was Raathi's first interview after he resigned from his post as party president.

The interviewer popped his first question the moment he settled down.

Interviewer: "The Nationalistic Party keeps on surprising us, doesn't it?"

Raathi (laughs softly): You should accept change. What we do, we do for the country...self-interest is the last thing on our minds."

Interviewer: "That's why the resignation?"

Raathi: "Just handover of responsibility. We promised a good and clean government to people and the party is striving to give that.... It's not a one man show! And never will be; we are a team! And before you ask, let me tell you that it's not a deliberate attempt to break any stereotype. Actually none of our actions are, but then media finds it interesting. As for us, we aspire to bring in a clean government! Period."

♌

Raathi had formed the Nationalistic Party with an aim to bring in clean corruption-free politics. Through his party, he wanted to bring change to the political system of the country. *That's what he had said!*

Nationalistic Party was as maligned as any other party in the country, but in the eyes of the public it maintained an image of a corruption free party! The price of that image was heavy. The media was being paid, people were removed, and huge money was exchanged.

There can never be clean politics. Ethical politics is a myth and clean governance is a chimerical dream. Ethics in politics are meant only for parliamentary speeches and election slogans.

Power corrupts! And politics is meant for power.

When I.M. Raathi, a former IAS officer, spoke about a corruption-free government, digging out this buried agenda, the media termed him a revolutionist. A true nationalist. In truth, Raathi was a shrewd man. A well-read, extensively travelled Indian diplomat who knew the nuances of running a government and the utmost requirement of the Indian people. He knew that even though people have accepted bureaucracy, bribery, and corruption as way of government operations, they are getting sick of it. With the expansion of the media in the country, people had started realizing that government was mishandling their tax money, in more ways than they already knew.

It was all statistics – GDP, GER, CAGR – all but numbers on papers! People can't see the change. Governments come and go, but status of the Indian people remains the same. Voter turnout began decreasing. People needed somebody to trust. They needed hope. The Nationalistic Party showed them a silver lining.

The human mind is not stubborn. It can be manipulated easily; all it needs is a slight glimpse of Elysian and an alpha to follow. It gets aligned to a cause and the herd starts following – following someone else's dreams and aspirations. I.M. Raathi had both credentials and the ability to be an alpha, to dissipate the seeds of hope and start a new following.

He had made his first public appearance as a politician, fifteen years back. Dressed in a stark white polo shirt and blue denims, he broke the typecast of Indian politicians. Raathi spoke in very simple language and never promised anything.

"Can a party promise a paradigm shift in the system in five years? It's nonsense! We are talking about a country with over a billion people here. Things cannot change drastically overnight! Not even in five years. Those who promise these things are not wizards!"

He paused for the laughter to subside and continued, "I am not a wizard! I am a normal person, and I know I can't do anything alone; nor can my party. I am tired of this narcissistic tendencies of parties – I, me myself – taking credit for everything.

"Our politicians don't think they are answerable to the masses. They are government servants; they are answerable! Not by showing their achievements in a full colour ad, but by giving services and not charging for it ..bribes, I mean," he paused and smiled.

"Unlike other parties, I can't promise a drastic change in five years, but I can promise a system," he continued. "Imagine a state of the art government building where you are attended to politely. Imagine a smiling government officer replying to your queries giving you a timeline and process for your work and ensuring that you are satisfied. Your request may take a long time to process, but when you will walk out of that building, you will be satisfied. Yes there is a system to ensure that and the Nationalistic Party can promise that system."

The crowd applauded.

Raathi took the nation by storm! Conventional party promises became a joke. The centre's competence was questioned. India witnessed such political drama for the first time, just as Raathi had planned. Who would have thought that behind those promises of a better tomorrow were intentions to destroy the future? Behind that empathetic saint-like eyes were devilish motives to attain power. Behind those futuristic vision was lust to control.

But then human eyes are capable of reflecting their own emotions in others. Frustrated Indians wanted hope and saw it in the Nationalistic Party.

Its majority win in Rajasthan assembly election was no surprise. The surprise was however Raathi's declaration of not becoming the Chief Minister.

"I am a simple man," Raathi spoke in the press conference, "I am a guide, not a leader. I know what's wrong and how to correct it, but I can't shout orders. A passive individual like me cannot run a government with aggression. While I will oversee all the processes, the post of CM will be held by Param V. Balacharan. He is an IIT, M alumnus. He hails from Tamil Nadu and has been settled here in Rajasthan for the last thirteen years. He gave up his job to join our party. He is young, self-driven, and motivated individual. Rajasthan needs a leader like him."

Param was neither motivated nor self-driven. He was, in fact, not even interested in joining politics, but did so because Armugham had asked him to. He didn't want to be CM either, but became so because Armugham asked him to. Armugham, on the other hand, was controlled by Raathi.

An academician with a Ph.D. in economics from Oxford, Armugham was among the founder members of the party. He even looped in huge Indian intelligentsia, which helped building the party's image and it grew exponentially. Armugham didn't have political aspirations himself. He just wanted to bring change, so when Raathi told him that he wanted Param to be the CM of Rajasthan, Armugham recoiled.

"I don't think Param is ready."

"All the more reason to do so, my brother," Raathi said in his ever so smooth voice. "He will not exploit his powers, he will listen. Besides we will be doing the work! All of it."

Armugham agreed reluctantly. Of course Param was just a face.

Five years and things remained as they were. Nothing changed; it wasn't supposed to. I.M. Raathi remained composed. Increasing apprehensions and opposition mudslinging could not deter him.

"What is the first step to clean and rearrange a closet? You de-clutter. Step one is taking out all the stuff from the closet. Now if someone walks past you, that person will find you sitting with a bigger mess. But you were cleaning out your closet. Years of dirt has piled up. Arranging a system took much longer time than we expected, but we are done now. You should be glad. Somebody has finally cleaned the closet!" Raathi spoke to the press before the next assembly election.

Anger mellowed, people saw hope again and the Nationalistic Party won the second time in a row. Param remained the face, Armugham a true loyalist and Raathi the controller.

♌

Interviewer: "What made you choose Mr Jamwal as the Prime Ministerial candidate over Mr Balacharan who has proven his administration skills in Rajasthan?"

Raathi (smiles): "Rajasthan is on its final phase of development. It needs Param's undivided attention. We have made a promise to the people of Rajasthan and we will do everything to keep that promise."

♌

When Armugham heard Raathi's aspirations for the Centre, he was taken aback, because Raathi proposed that Ashwin Jamwal would be the Prime Ministerial candidate from the Nationalistic Party. What shocked him more was that Raathi would also give away his post as party president.

"Ten years back you told me you trusted me the most," Armugham said to Raathi. They both were sitting in the party HQ.

"I still do. Why are you saying that?" Raathi replied.

Of course he knew why. Not ten, but eleven years back Raathi had told Armugham that he trusted him and would want only his loyalist to seat an important chair. Param was chosen as Prime Ministerial candidate in the last General Assembly elections. He failed miserably. Param was neither a good orator, nor a leader. He was only a puppet controlled by Armugham.

Power is addictive. The Nationalistic Party had better chances in the Lok Sabha than the last time. If at all they won, Armugham would like his puppet to be the PM.

"You have to understand Armugham," Raathi stressed. "The Centre is a different ballgame. We failed the last time and I took all the blame. But honestly, we did not offer a great PM to the country. Besides, people of Rajasthan are getting frustrated. We have to work a lot! Param has to do something in the state. We can't fail this time—"

"We haven't done anything in the last eleven years!"

"Precisely!" Raathi nodded. "We can't fail. And besides you can't deny, if somebody has credentials to be a PM, it is Ashwin. He is very popular!"

"Just because he looks good."

"Looks added to the popularity, yes! But he is our best shot. He is an immaculate speaker. He has proven his mettle in all our campaigns. He is a born leader."

Armugham looked at him as if Raathi was looking for a born leader. The only reason Ashwin was chosen was because of his blind belief in Raathi. If Raathi wanted control at the centre, Ashwin was the best bet.

"But why the party president-ship?" Armugham asked

"Just a designation so that people fascinated with grades take him more seriously. Let's not forget he is just a face…"

♌

Interviewer: "Mr Jamwal's fan base is equal to fans of all the politicians combined. As per our data, Mr Jamwal has exceeded your popularity even in the state of Rajasthan where people used to worship you!"

Raathi (smiles): "Count me out of the social networking race (laughs). I don't want to be popular. I am happy the way I am and I am happy that people have accepted Ashwin."

After the interview was over, Raathi slowly moved towards the glass table. The interview SOP and schedule was still lying there. He stared at it for some time and then smashed his fist on the table in frustration. The glass cracked, cutting his hands deeply. He was losing it!

2

The members of Nationalistic Party had gathered at suite number 1307 of a five-star hotel in Cochin. They were planning the agenda for a rally the next day. There were fifteen odd people from the marketing, strategy, and analytics team in that four hundred square feet of space. Most of the young members were sitting on the floor, because there weren't enough chairs. The veterans such as Raathi, Armugham, Param, also Sanjay Tripathi and Uday Bopanna, the party secretaries, took their places on the couch.

Ashwin was sitting at the study table on the far left. He was typing something on his laptop. Two young members from analytics were leaning over him and giving occasional inputs.

Finally he stopped typing and gave the print command. As the printer whirred, he stretched himself on the chair. He was exhausted. He must have typed for two hours. The Nationalistic Party was not popular in the south and they had to be very clear with the agenda of the rallies to make it a success.

Sanya, the youngest party member handed over the prints to Raathi.

"Here, these are the points of the agenda: the case references, facts and the issues that need to be addressed. Everything is mentioned in bullets under separate heads," Ashwin said getting up and moving to the couch where the veterans were sitting.

Raathi took the paper and began reading it. Ashwin stood behind him to observe his expressions. Raathi looked pleased with the content.

"Well?" Ashwin asked.

"You don't need our opinions. Do you?" Armugham replied instead.

Ashwin looked at him. Armugham was as expressionless as ever and he couldn't make out whether it was a sarcastic remark or humble appreciation.

"Of course I need your opinions and feedback. Especially now, *this* is your place, you know how we can drive the campaign." He moved towards the study table

"As I said in the interview the other day, you guys have made me.... I will always need you to guide me!" he added, perching himself on the study table. He could see everyone in the room.

"Yet, 'The Great Political Debate' did not have a single point, which *we* had discussed!" Armugham spoke, tilting his head. We had discussed everything from the party manifesto and UP crisis, to industry policies. But you talked about foreign policies!"

Sanya looked at Ashwin and sent a message with heart emoticons, to another colleague in that room, who replied with an angry emoji and 'my crush first!' And with that, the exchange of no brainer messages started, involving almost every young member in that room. They were oblivious to the tension among veterans.

"Because the debate did not start the way it should have!" Ashwin replied irritated. "The opposition was ready with its counterattack on industry policy and UP crisis. The moderator was ready with his own set of questions on these issues. I had got the information before, so I talked about something, which was equally relevant, but our opponent was not ready with facts to counter it. I thought it went well. According to the people's verdict, we won that debate!" he replied, getting down from the table. "I didn't know I have to massage everyone's ego here. I thought we were a team and all my decisions will not be questioned," he added acerbically. He could sense the discordance in the party.

"You did the right thing, Ashwin," Raathi said in his ever so comforting voice. "It gave us the upper hand in the debate. All your decisions have been good for the party. We trust you with the position. I am sure Armugham will agree."

"I do!" Armugham said looking at Ashwin and then straight at the wall. "I didn't mean to question your ability. I am just paranoid, as you said, it's *my* place. I am answerable to every commitment, you will make in the rally. I just don't want to sweat, in case you decide to say something we did not discuss."

"I know. I am sorry for the outburst!" Ashwin replied smiling wanly. "I guess I am tired."

"Don't be tired now!" Raathi said sharply. "We have to discuss the campaign plan. We had a very poor turnout in Coimbatore, and Cochin is also looking weak."

"I know!" Param spoke for the first time. "It had rained heavily a day before in Coimbatore, yet the supporters came!"

"Supporters should come, even if it's raining at the time of the rally!" Raathi said looking at Ashwin for support, "Your marketing should be so effective"

"I agree!" Ashwin replied looking at the marketing team. They were all glued to their phones. "Though, I would not like to give a speech, in the rain."

"Me neither!" Armugham replied. "It's difficult to talk with all that water on your face. Besides, the microphone converts your voice into some robotic sound. It's scary."

Everybody laughed.

"Got it!" Raathi replied wiping his glasses. "I thought I made a good point there."

"You did! The team has made a good campaign plan," Ashwin said looking at the team again. "They are planning to develop some applications for phones, a simulation game like Farmville where the user will be in charge of a small territory. Then we will use VR to give the user a glimpse into an ideal India—"

"VR?? Farm?" Raathi asked baffled.

Ashwin laughed. "Virtual Reality and Farmville! Never mind. Thanks for reminding me about the marketing plan, Inderji. We will share the entire plan first thing tomorrow. I will go get some fresh air," he said starting for the door and called out. "Seriously Dhiren. Look up from the phone, already."

Dhiren was head marketing and PR.

"Call the team; we will discuss the plan outside."

Dhiren got up hurriedly and dusted his pants. His team also stood up while Ashwin held the door for them.

"What's up with your phones? Please tell me you were working on a marketing plan."

"Yes sir! We were!" Sanya spoke almost immediately.

It was an hour before midnight when they went for a stroll in the garden of the hotel. It was very quiet and tranquil. A perfect ambience for a creative discussion. They must have talked about the marketing strategy for over an hour. The team then began craving for something which stimulates creative nerves – tea and cigarettes!

"You know there is a tea shop just opposite the hotel," spoke Bikash. He had recently joined the Nationalistic Party after quitting a high paying job.

"Then let's go out!" Ashwin said.

"But sir... you?" Dhiren asked surprised. "I mean security?"

"It's not far away, is it?" Ashwin asked Bikash.

"Just outside!" he replied.

"Then let's go! I hate this hotel's tea, and more than that I hate paying a bomb for it!"

The tea shop was hardly fifteen feet away from the hotel gate. The shop owner made good money selling tea to bored office employees on night shifts. There was nobody at the tea shop, though. As the shop owner began making the tea, the group settled on old wooden benches. In a moment the entire street was filled with excited noises from the marketing team. They were telling Ashwin about their goof ups in the political arena. Ashwin could relate to their miseries for he had faced a similar situation when he was younger.

"Some stereotypes are here to stay!" Ashwin said looking down. Sanya was smoking. He was still not comfortable seeing a young girl smoke.

"You will all learn! Dressing up, communication with your seniors, communication in public and dealing with the media. After a while it will all come naturally, you won't have to force it!" he noticed his shoe laces were untied.

"We are from the corporate world. I guess it makes it harder for us! Adjustment must be easier for you though," Dhiren said.

"Maybe," Ashwin said, bending down to tie his shoe laces. While he was at it, he saw the glass jar in the tea shop shatter to pieces. He was about to get up when he heard a thud. He smelled burnt wood. He moved his eyes and saw a hole on right leg of the bench. A hole that can be made only by a bullet!

They were being attacked

Ashwin heard a few more ricocheting sounds. He crouched, calling out to Sanya to do the same. Too late. She fell off the bench; a bullet had hit her right temple. Suddenly, Ashwin felt a warm sensation around his waist. He touched it with his fingers and felt something moist. *Blood.* He needed a shelter to hide!

The assaulter was firing aimlessly, so he understood that the assaulter couldn't see him properly in the dark. That helped. Ashwin began crawling towards the tea shop slowly. He slid under the platform used for making tea and keeping biscuits and cigarettes, and laid down on his back. Ashwin thought of his team and regretted his decision of leaving the hotel. A moment ago, they were all laughing and having a good time. Now Sanya was dead. He saw Dhiren's body lying next to her. He didn't know whether he was dead or alive. He didn't see Bikash and Sandeep. He hoped they made it to a safe place!

The muffled sound stopped. Ashwin could hear footsteps, the assaulter has stopped firing and was slowly approaching the tea shop.

Ashwin held his breath; the burner overhead was still on fire. It had kerosene! A shot at that burner and Ashwin Jamwal would be history. The assaulter was only three feet away.

Two feet.

The assaulter stopped suddenly and Ashwin braced himself. He could smell his death. The iron sweet smell of the blood mixing with wet ground beneath. The assaulter did not fire. Instead Ashwin heard him say 'seri' several times. He must have got a call. To Ashwin's surprise, the assaulter turned and began leaving. Ashwin heard the sound of footsteps going farther.

He inched himself to catch a glimpse of his running assaulter and all he could see was the left hand. It had only two fingers – the little finger and the thumb. Ashwin was pretty sure he had seen that hand before.

He then heard more footsteps. The alert tea shop owner had rushed to the hotel and brought help. Members of the party, hotel officials and security staff crowded that area.

He heard Armugham's voice.

"Ashwin's here! Oh shit. He's been hit," Armugham cried leaning over Ashwin. "How are you feeling?" he asked him with concern and then called out, "There is a lot of blood. He is still conscious! Somebody call the ambulance please!" He turned to Ashwin again, "Can you hear me, Ashwin? Stay with me."

Ashwin wasn't listening; he remembered he had seen his assaulter in Coimbatore, talking to Armugham.

![Knight chess piece symbol]

Arun Deb's heart was beating faster with every step he was taking towards the ICU where Ashwin was admitted. It had been been three days since the attack. If TV news was to be believed, his condition was not improving. Arun knocked on the door softly and immediately opened it. Ashwin was lying on the bed, attached to various machines; with an IV line inserted in his right arm. A young doctor was monitoring a machine.

"Hello!" the doctor said turning, "Mr Deb?"

"Yes! How is he now?" Arun asked, uneasy with the remittent beeps from the machines.

"He is fine, sir."

"Is he out of danger?" Arun asked, feeling silly asking such a question in an ICU, but he had to. Though he was not part of the political arena, he knew how it worked. Information is tweaked, modified, and even hidden from the public, just for self-interest. Ashwin may in reality have nothing more than a bruise, which was propagated as a life-threatening condition. The Nationalistic Party was in the news for the last three days, getting sympathy and support. That is what it wanted.

"Please tell me the truth!" Arun said firmly.

"He is alright, sir. He was out of danger twenty-one hours after admission, even less, but we were told—"

"I know. Political mind-games."

"I am telling you because of your relationship with Mr Jamwal and…umm…your profile."

"Thanks," Arun replied. He had announced his arrival to the hospital staff clearly stating his designation – DIG, Indore. The hospital shoved the youngest doctor forward to face him. That's how it works. If it went okay, it's team effort; if something goes wrong, the youngest, most inexperienced faces the consequences.

"Can I talk to him?" he asked.

"He is resting…" the doctor hesitated.

"Don't worry, I will keep it short. Good? And please give us some privacy," Arun said moving towards Ashwin's bed.

The doctor nodded and left.

Arun puts his face closer to Ashwin and called his name softly several times. Ashwin stirred and blinked. He was heavily sedated.

"Arun? Here?"

"How are you feeling?" Arun asked dragging a chair and sitting on it.

"How come you are here?" Ashwin asked, his voice hoarse.

"The news channels have been talking about the attack since the last three days; that you are fighting for your life. Your phone wasn't reachable and that 'Raathi of yours' told me nothing and disconnected the phone while I was still talking!"

Ashwin smiled weakly.

"You are smiling?" Arun said faking anger, though he was relieved to see Ashwin smiling.

"That Raathi of yours," Ashwin pointed.

Arun followed a peculiar naming convention in distress; it ended with 'of yours'.

Arun smiled back. "You are out of danger. Do you know that?"

Ashwin nodded weakly, "Inderji told me. It is best if we do not disclose it yet. It will give our assassin some moments of anxiety."

"Manipulation!"

Ashwin ignored Arun's comment and continued, "Sanya is dead. You know Dhiren is fighting for his life? He became a father only few weeks ago. Bikash was hit on his legs. He may never walk properly again and Sandeep will be on slings for months. You know they took bullets meant for me? You are calling it manipulation? That's how it works. If I am out of bed and back on track in a day's time, nobody will talk about these people even for an hour! If I weren't hit at all, you would have found only a ticker on a news channel reading 'four members of Nationalistic Party attacked: one dead; one critical.' Nothing more!"

"By lying about your condition, you guys may get sympathy, but people who love you get worried," Arun added with irritation.

"You can think as you please. That girl could have died an unknown death. At least now people know about her and her qualities," Ashwin paused for some time. "I am only justifying myself, right?"

"Maybe, doesn't matter. You are okay and that's important! Call your mother and talk to her when you can. Okay? She is traumatized. I stopped her from coming here. I felt I should come and see you first."

Ashwin nodded weakly.

"But the fact is somebody did attack you," Arun said. "And we don't know who? You know, the Kerala Police interrogated that tea shop owner. It was dark and the assassin was firing from a distance so he was of no help."

"I have seen the assassin."

"You what?" Arun sat up in shock.

"I saw him in Coimbatore. He was talking to Armugham!"

"Oh great, just great!" Arun said excitedly. "What were they saying?"

"Don't know. They were talking in Tamil!"

"Have you told anyone?"

"No."

"Great. Don't, till we find out more."

♌

Thiteen days later, I.M. Raathi was sitting alone in his living room, admiring himself on the news channel. The media had done a good job. He was talking about the party position after the ambush.

"We have lost our daughter, and our beloved president had to fight for his life. It is a hard time for the party, more for me; Ashwin is more than just a president. He is my son! They thought, by attacking him, they can actually break us! Well they are wrong. God is with us. Nobody can harm us. In fact, we are stronger than before. If we are a threat, it means we are good."

Impeccable and charming as ever.

Pretty narcissistic, but Raathi could never get tired of admiring himself. He called out to his maid and asked her to fill the bowl of peanuts, while he poured himself a drink. His phone rang.

Unknown number.

Raathi checked the time; it was half past eleven at night. He got a very few calls on this number. He picked up the call and listened in silence to the voice at the other end. Then as if in slow motion, the phone fell from his hand

The call just told him about the death of underworld don, Murugan Swamy. The police had discovered the dead body in a room of a plush hotel in Dubai. Raathi had paid Murugan Swamy two crores to kill Ashwin Jamwal. Mururgan Swamy was dead. And worse, somebody knew.

Raathi got up from his chair, staggered and fell.

♌

When Arun's mobile rang during the early hours, he initially mixed the ringtone with the sequence in his dream. Only after a while he realized that nobody was singing. It was his phone! Groggily, he put it on his ears, with his eyes still closed, but the news on the phone made him fully awake.

"What? When?" he said, sitting up.

His wife jolted up from sleep and blinked. She then noticed the phone and turned away.

"Where did you find his body? Can you get more information?" He fired two questions at once and listened intently. "Well, I will speak to TN police directly. Thanks for filling me in," he said and hung up. But first I have to talk to Ashwin, he said to himself

"What happened?" his wife asked.

"Ashwin's two fingered assassin is dead," Arun replied somewhat lost.

♌

Ashwin folded the paper shut and kept it along with other newspapers lying on the centre table. He was in the meeting room of the party HO in South Delhi, for a meeting with the PR team to discuss the media coverage of their campaign. The party had paid the print media a huge sum for front page coverage on the '*Clean us, clean government*' campaign started by the party across India. It did not happen.

The front page was all about Murugan Swamy.

Ashwin shook his head in disappointment, "What a waste of funds and efforts."

"No sir! We don't have to pay the media again!" Rahul, from Dhiren's team spoke hurriedly. Dhiren was recuperating and Rahul was taking care of PR in his absence.

"Of course we won't!" Ashwin said firmly, "I wasn't talking about that. I was talking about the cost of the campaign. The workers have to stage it again!"

"I spoke to the campaign coordinator and he said they will do it again," Junaid, another team member pitched in.

"No matter how hard you try, you can never get the same enthusiasm the next day." Ashwin pursed his lips, "Who the hell is this Murugan Swamy?" he added.

"Sir, he is the dreaded underworld don—" Junaid began but Ashwin cut him short.

"I know who he is. Fuck him. He really chose a bad day to die!" Ashwin added in frustration. Almost immediately he realized, five years back, he could not even think of making a remark such as this. But here he was, cursing a dreaded don because he was killed on the day of his campaign, and media had to cover his death instead of their propaganda. Pragmatic morality?

He remembered a conversation with his father on Julius Caesar's last words: 'et tu, Brute?' The position and the power to control changes an individual's behaviour and outlook and he may end up doing the same things he protested against once.

By the time you become PM, crossing all the hurdles and going through hardship after being manipulated and controlled numerous times, you truly become indifferent to the oath and promises you made to yourself in the beginning. When you become the ultimate authority, you only enjoy that power to control. Et tu, Brute!

Ashwin's phone rang. It was Arun.

"I have a bad news!" Arun said.

"I am not getting any good news these days. Nothing unusual," Ashwin replied moving to the far end of the room.

"You know Murugan Swamy is dead? Killed?"

"Yes I know!" Ashwin said sulkily, "It's all over the news!"

"Do you know who he was?" Arun asked.

"Yes, he has a full coverage in all the newspapers! The way they are portraying a criminal and glorifying his crimes, it may influence many young kids to follow his footsteps. A war martyr doesn't get a full pager! Media today, I am telling you, is such a waste," Ashwin said angrily.

"Okay!" Arun said empathetically, "You calm down and listen to me carefully. Your two fingered assassin was Murugan Swamy's aide."

"What?"

"And the bad news is that he is dead too. He was murdered a few days ago. Tamil Nadu police found his body in a sewer in Nammakkal."

♌

Armugham got up from his chair and began pacing pensively. His steps were heavy. He was in the Delhi marketing office which was an old bungalow, temporarily made into the office. Ashwin had called him last night and arranged for a one-to-one here, but he was early. With every passing minute, Armugham was getting more anxious.

The office was deserted till afternoon. The marketing team was fairly young; the volunteers were all college goers. They only worked on campaign activities after their classes. The core team never used the place mainly because it was small and way too cluttered.

Armugham examined the room. This room must have been a study earlier, it now served more as a storeroom for the marketing collaterals. Stacks of pamphlets were everywhere. There was little room to walk. The desk had a layer of dust, and the only two chairs looked old and rusted. Armugham looked at his watch and sat on the chair again, cursing himself for the anxiety, but then the coldness in Ashwin's voice had told him that something was terribly wrong.

After a while, Armugham heard a car by the gate. His heart raced and he felt a chill at the back of his neck.

Ashwin pushed the heavy door and entered the room. It smelled of fresh ink. He sighed and moved towards the desk, without looking at Armugham. Armugham remain seated. Ashwin dusted the table and positioned himself next to it to face Armugham. He noticed that for the first time Armugham looked nervous and threatened. He didn't like it.

"How's your health Ashwin?" Armugham spoke after a while.

"I am better," Ashwin replied frowning. He hadn't expected Armugham to be cowering nervously. After the news of Murugan Swamy's death, Arun had allowed him to confront Armugham. He even asked Ashwin to take precautions. So, not only did Ashwin come with security staff in plain clothes, for guarding the premises, he himself was carrying a small pocket knife.

"Why this... unscheduled meeting? I was supposed to go to TN today," Armugham said, his eyes moving rapidly.

"I wanted to ask you a thing or two," Ashwin said and mounted himself on the table.

"Please go ahead," Armugham said moving his chair a little farther from Ashwin.

"I just want honest replies from you!"

"I am an academician and will remain so. I don't believe in prevaricating."

"Spare me the English!"

"I will be honest. Please ask," Armugham said trying to stay calm though his heart was beating so fast, that it could burst.

"I may be new to politics but I'm sure you agree that I know how to get things done around here."

Armugham nodded, his mind confused. Did he call him for a self-praise session?

"And that's why I play an instrumental role in party alliances," Ashwin continued. *Yes, a self-praise session.*

"I get inside information on opposition's strategies, pre-election campaign scandals easily. In fact, I knew the topic of the political debate beforehand and..." Ashwin paused briefly, "I know who ordered my assassination."

"What? You know who is behind the attack?"

"Yes," Ashwin replied curtly. "You!"

"What?" Armugham felt the ground slipping away from under his feet. If Ashwin was blaming him for the attack, that meant he had strong evidence against him. But how?

"Me? Why Kanna?" he blurted, clutching the armrest of the chair to steady himself.

"Because, sadly for you, I saw the assassin," Ashwin said controlling his anger. "I saw him that night when he tried to kill me, and a few days before in Coimbatore. I noticed that he was following us, but I ignored him. To me, he was harmless." Ashwin paused briefly and continued in an even harsher tone. "You know why I thought he was harmless? Because he was talking to you. The so called academician and not politician – Mr Armugham."

"What?" he replied, shifting nervously on his chair. "Who was talking to me?"

"The two-fingered assassin. Dammit!" Ashwin said getting down from the table. "The assassin was tipped to kill me in the hotel garden, where there's enough light to aim and shoot, but then we went to the tea shop and he failed. And now I am standing here with you in a tete-a tete with a weapon around my waist and armed personnel guarding my back. There is no way out for you, Armugham."

"What are you saying?" Armugham replied weakly. He started feeling a mild pain in his chest.

"There is no point denying it!" Ashwin said hitting a stack of flyers and letting the coloured papers fly all over the place.

"Do you think I can plan something as conniving as this? Your murder?" Armugham spoke breathing heavily.

"I don't think. I know!" Ashwin replied with conviction in his voice, his mind a little confused. Can a bespectacled academician plan something like this?

"I know you were close to Murugan Swamy. Don't even try to deny it!"

Armugham did not reply so he continued, "Well! My assassin was Murugan Swamy's man! Now, does that make sense?"

Armugham and Murugan were Tamil refugees from Sri Lanka. Their friendship started at refugee camps in Tamil Nadu. Murugan had always helped Armugham, monetarily and otherwise. For the world, Murugan was a merciless killer and an underworld don. But for Armugham, his thambi, best friend and a confidant.

"Murugan Swamy only helped us in getting the outside support in last LA election, otherwise the Nationalistic Party could have never formed a government in Rajasthan for the third time,' Armugham said looking straight at Ashwin. "Murugan was special. The world celebrated his death," Armugham continued, "But a part of me died that day."

"I know," Ashwin said. "How much did you pay him to kill me?"

"I did not pay him or anybody to kill you!" Armugham cried exasperatedly, his breathing getting a little erratic. "Why would I want to kill you?"

Ashwin shrugged, "Maybe because you wanted Param to be the PM and not me".

"Param can't run a shop, let alone a country! Why would I want him to be a PM?" Words were coming out with difficulty.

"If I am out of the picture, Param is sure to get the party president chair. As such the party is scoring pretty well now. With my death, it will get sympathy votes and our chances of winning the general election will increase; which means Param could become PM. And it's no secret that you pull his strings."

"It's true that I was close to Murugan Swamy. And it's also true that Param listens to everything I say," Armugham said slowly, talking was hurting him. "But your 'so called informants' did not give you the correct information. I would never do a thing to harm you, and if you are behind Murugan's death, you've made a mistake!"

"What are you rambling?" Ashwin said sitting up straight. He was furious. "I wish I was behind his death but I would never kill him because he was just carrying out orders *you gave.* I would rather have *you* suffer," he said under his breath.

Armugham began feeling weak, "Your suspicion is enough suffering. Believe me, I can never conspire against you. I....ud....dah..."

His last words slurred off his mouth incoherently. He rested his head on the back rest. His throat was making a gurgling sound. With partially opened eyes, Armugham saw Ashwin getting alarmed and rushing to his side. He knew he had pushed himself too far today. He was getting a heart attack, but ignored it because he just wanted Ashwin to believe him.

Armugham had always liked Ashwin, but Ashwin never saw that. Armugham has found his son in Ashwin, but Ashwin never felt that. That day Ashwin accused him of a felony a father would never commit.

Armugham was mumbling something when he saw Ashwin dashing towards him with concern in his eyes. Genuine concern. Ashwin was saying something to him, but Armugham wasn't listening. He raised his left hand slightly and Ashwin took it immediately.

The last sensation which Armugham felt was warmth, which only a son can give to his father. He closed his eyes.

![chess knight symbol]

Ranjan Saxena settled himself on the thick armchair as he waited for Param to arrive. He was at Param's private bungalow in Manesar, Gurgaon. He had been told that Param was on his way. Ranjan looked at his watch – 12: 45 a.m. He smiled to himself. He was still fresh, ready to live another phase of his life. Twenty-four hours! Too much and too little; too much for daytime activities, that are covered in the media; too little for actions that happen behind; the actions that define him.

Ranjan Saxena was Minister for Health and Family Welfare and Param was the senior member of a contesting party. That morning Ranjan had mocked the Nationalistic Party agenda and called them novices and indifferent to the ground realities of villages in India.

"They are traitors, they talk foreign policies. Children in India are suffering from malnourishment; infant mortality rate is going higher. Death during childbirth is going higher. During such times when we should only concentrate on providing better hospital services and infrastructure here, the Nationalistic Party is talking about strengthening foreign relations. They are but pimps to foreign countries. They will sell us to them!"

At night, he was at Param's bungalow for a very private conversation.

Ranjan Saxena was a powerful man. He had been charged with criminal offences more than just once, but he would come out clean every time. The government had been accused for intrusting an important ministry to a man with such a record, but Saxena was resourceful.

Politicians are known for misuse of power and corruption, but behind their political visage is a back story – of loss, betrayal and hardship.

Ranjan Saxena had hated politics twenty-seven years back. Particularly because his elder son Akhil became a student politician and refused to follow the legacy of his parents, who were established lawyers. In 1988, Akhil was murdered by the opposition party.

Ranjan made a secret vow to himself to punish his son's killer, but his twenty years of legal expertise couldn't bring justice to his own son. After two years of constant struggle with the legal system, Ranjan gave up and joined the party his son was supporting, only because they promised justice for him and his son.

Politics is such a bitch, it gives you pleasure, but takes away all you have.

By the time Ranjan reached a position to avenge his son's death, he didn't want to. That would be a political suicide. He couldn't afford that, after he had tasted power.

Power is addictive, power corrupts.

Param arrived and was apologetic. "I had to go to Suresh Anna's house," he said moving over to the bar and making a drink. He was about to sit when he saw Ranjan without a glass. "Oh! I am sorry, I didn't ask you. What will you have?"

Ranjan shook his head, "Later. Suresh Anna? Armugham?"

"Yes!" Param sighed and sat across on the couch.

"Sad. He couldn't make it. He was a fighter. How long was he on artificial support?" Ranjan asked.

"Ten days," Param replied softly, looking at the rim of his glass.

"I am sorry. You were very close to him," Ranjan said and meant it too.

"So were you!" Param smiled briefly.

"Not personally!" Ranjan smiled. "Or publically. What was between me and Armugham was very professional. It was strategic; a good symbiotic relationship. It strengthened after Nandi's death," Ranjan paused and then added. "We sure are losing friends this year!"

Param sighed, "We are. And yet we cannot lament," he said looking at Ranjan.

"Couldn't agree more. And even though we politicians are called stone-hearted, we have something that beats. We too have that angel sitting on our shoulder telling us what's right—"

"And we ignore her."

Ranjan smiled and continued, "We know what is right or wrong. What we should do and what not. We have an angel on one shoulder and a devil sitting on the other. Sadly, the devil is louder. But when we go to bed at night and all the voices fade, we hear our heartbeat."

"Profound. Very philosophical, especially for a lawyer turned politician, and you are not even drunk yet."

"I think I should," Ranjan said getting up and going to the bar. "What I am trying to say is that we politicians are humans too. As for Armugham, he had his own vices. He could have slept with Sumona for party funds, or paid heavily to the media pimp to hide his asset details. He misused his power more than just once. But he was a human," he paused as he cautiously poured his drink from a heavy bottle and then spoke. "So, it may seem like a heartless profession but being human, we all are controlled by our own devils and angels."

He sat back on the armchair. "I know there have been differences in your party ever since Ashwin became the president; founder members and veterans are not pleased, even though Ashwin is a strong leader. Had Armugham listened to his angel and not confronted Ashwin, he may have still been alive, but then his devil took over."

"You are wrong! Anna's devil would never take over when it comes to Ashwin."

"Oh! I thought he disliked Ashwin."

"On the contrary, Anna saw his son in Ashwin! His real son's name was Ashwini Krishnan, who died a day before his seventh birthday. It was an accident in the kitchen and Anna blamed his wife. They did not separate legally but never stayed together after that. Anna loved his son!

Then after two decades he met Ashwin. He believed that if his son had been alive, he would look exactly like Ashwin."

Param had his drink in one gulp and cringed, "He liked only one person in the world and never told him."

"I always thought *you* are the only person he *liked,*" Ranjan said.

"He liked me, but not that way!" Param replied sadly. "I was a student. Nothing more." He sighed. "Ashwin was his son."

"But what happened in the conference? Armugham was okay before that."

"Ashwin thought Anna has planned his assassination earlier this month," Param said going to the bar. "Ashwin called for an urgent meeting at the marketing office when Anna was scheduled to go to Cochin; he asked him to cancel that. Anna called me and said he could sense the coldness in Ashwin's voice. He was a wise man, Ranjan; he sensed everything from that call."

"Armugham was a wise man. It's such a loss," Ranjan said sadly.

Param nodded.

"Suresh Armugham was an academician. He was getting tired of politics. He wasn't meant for it, yet he could never come out of it. Politics is like an abysmal pit; you can get inside it, but can never come out," Param said. "His conscience was killing him, and the last thing his heart needed was an accusation from the person he considered his son."

"Silly emotions. Who was Ashwin to him?" Ranjan said looking absently at the wall.

"No one!" Param said furiously, 'but then Anna was always protective about him."

"Protective?" Ranjan said after a moment of silence. "Protective about Ashwin? Why would a man like Ashwin need protection? He was pretty powerful himself."

"You don't become powerful just like that!" Param said bitterly.

"Come on. We all know Ashwin has worked hard. He knows what to do and how." Ranjan said getting up. "You want something?" he asked Param, noticing his empty glass.

"Scotch with ice."

Ranjan nodded.

"There are no doubts about Ashwin's talent," Param continued watching Ranjan making their drinks. "But then there must be a hundred equally talented politicians in this country right now…with the same levels of network, same skills. Like Nandi, like yourself. Don't *you* know how things work here? Don't *you* have connections? Staged sympathies, private parties, you also know everything! Yet in popularity and power, Ashwin Jamwal is way ahead."

"Is it? Even in power?" Ranjan asked handing the glass to Param.

"Yes. And a man cannot rise to such power in such short a time on his own. He then makes enemies."

"He has been here for a long time now!"

"Less than a decade!" Param added irritated. "I don't know why you are defending him."

"I am not! It's hard to believe.'"

"Ok. Tell me how much time did it take you to become secretary from a party worker at the regional level?"

"Forever. Don't talk about it!" Ranjan muttered.

"Exactly! He became party president in less than a decade! I feel somebody is harnessing him."

"There are exceptions."

"Eh? Of what?" Param asked confused.

"Of people rising to power and popularity in a short time, like Surendra Narula of the Trikone Dhwaj Party."

"How can you even compare Ashwin with Narula? Firstly, TDP was Narula's own party. Secondly, his popularity was short-lived and nothing compared to Ashwin. And thirdly, he had no power. The party was out of the radar in three years. Narula made a fool of himself."

"Why do I smell jealousy?"

Param was annoyed. "Why would I be jealous? I do not have any political ambitions. I took the front seat because I had been asked to do so; because, I was that disciple who'd follow the teacher's instructions. We, Tamils, are like that; we worship our idols and listen to them."

"But then except for Armugham, who would harness Ashwin?" Ranjan said after a while.

Param shook his head, "Given a chance, Armugham would have removed Ashwin from the political arena," he finished his drink.

"Raathi?"

"Could be, I don't know. Raathi is a shrewd man; he must have seen something in Jamwal because I have heard that Raathi convinced Ashwin to leave a perfectly good job and join the party. Why did Ashwin agree? It's a mystery. He was the DC in Udaipur."

"That sounds fishy," Ranjan said astonished. "Raathi must have made an offer he couldn't refuse…Like party president post or the PM candidature?"

"Could be…" Param shrugged. "But then trust me, Raathi did not groom him the way he groomed me. In fact Raathi paid attention to him only after he rose to popularity, thanks to the social media. He has voice and young people listen to him; Raathi got a dynamic leader in his party without even working on the same. Raathi is a shrewd man." Param sighed. "He has his own plans. We are just his puppets. He is very calculated; everything has a reason. From the inception of the party to breaking stereotypes, making me chief minister or giving the president's post to Ashwin," Param said getting up for another drink.

"Armugham may have been protecting Ashwin from Raathi. He could have known Raathi's real intentions."

"I agree. Besides, Ashwin turned out to be different from Raathi's regular underlings. Better than Raathi, in fact."

"I guess it was like Mary Shelly's Frankenstein. Raathi was threatened by the magnanimity of his product."

"Though he shouldn't be. Ashwin could be a strong force himself, but he adores Raathi. He may have a voice louder than us; but at the end of the day, he is also a puppet!" Param said. "Raathi always wanted to have a strong leader in the party. Ashwin is his horse for the 'Ashavmedha yagna'," he said and smiled.

"I got it," Ranjan chuckled. "He is the best horse that will be sacrificed in the end. But then Ashwin has his own political ambitions and that's where the trouble started. Armugham must have foreseen it, that's why he was protecting him."

"Maybe. Once, high on alcohol, Anna told me he would do everything under the sun of Ashwin's aspirations. That was before Ashwin joined us. Ten years back."

"Ten years back? You remembered?"

"Never forgotten."

♌

Back in the car, Ranjan mulled over the conversation he had had with Param and chuckled to himself. A small variation here and there, but he had known the whole story of the Nationalistic Party. Param had only validated it.

Param had also blurted the truth Ranjan wanted to hear. Ashwin did not become powerful on his own. He had been jacked up to this position.

Ashwin finished his tea and carefully placed the cup on the saucer. Even before he could start drinking his tea, Arun had told him that the tea-set was very expensive, and he should be careful with it. So all along, Ashwin used both hands to hold the cup, more as a playful gesture than precaution. Irrespective of the stature of the person in a society, one can never be formal at an old friend's place.

The pre-election campaign was at its last phase and Ashwin was in Bhopal for the same. Arun has been posted in Bhopal for the last two years, so he invited Ashwin over for dinner.

"So how is Mai now?" Ashwin asked the moment the cup made a safe landing on the table.

"She is better. The doctor had advised more morning walks and less sweets," Arun said smiling. "And both are equally difficult to fulfil."

He laughed. He was meeting Ashwin alone after a long time in *his* bungalow and Ashwin was relaxed for a change. Just like old times

"Some romance she has with sweets, especially rasgulla," Ashwin said laughing

"God! How many can she eat? She doesn't get tired!" Arun smiled. "And how is Uncle? Quiet as usual?"

"Yep, like he is not there!"

Ashwin laughed.

"They are so proud of you," Arun said quietly. "Especially Mai."

"During my last visit, she got up early just to make me her signature machhar jhol! Of all the things, I miss her macchar jhol the most."

"I better change the menu for dinner!" Arun's wife said, getting up.

"What? Why?" Arun asked.

"Oh! I don't want you guys to compare my cooking with Mai's!"

The men laughed and began talking about their childhood in Allahabad. Arun would occasionally make jokes about his married life and fatherhood and would be immediately rebuked by his wife. This light-hearted conversation went on till they finished dinner. After that Arun took Ashwin to the balcony for a smoke.

For a few moments, both of them smoked in silence. Arun then noticed that Ashwin was smiling to himself.

"What's so funny?" Arun asked.

"I am smoking, that's funny." Ashwin laughed, expelling the smoke.

"Yeah, you smoke with me. So?"

"I smoke *only* with you," Ashwin said then whispered, "Nobody knows. Nobody should know!"

Arun laughed. He understood that Ashwin had to maintain a public image, especially when they were so close to the election date. At this point all the parties were being monitored, and even the slightest mistake could be disastrous for the party and the candidate. This was the time when all politicians put up their best faces forward.

"Only a few weeks now, then you will be PM of the nation," Arun spoke.

"The Nationalistic Party will not form the government this year!" Ashwin said matter of factly.

"What?"

"I read the poll predictions. Did the analysis, worked on the alliances. We won't get enough seats!" he replied stubbing the cigarette in the ashtray.

"Not even with the alliances?" Arun asked shocked.

"We have very little in our kitty and even with the current and expected alliances we would not be able to form the government," he replied moving to the iron chairs.

"What about the biggies? What if you get looped in with the biggie?" Arun said following Ashwin.

"I will not be PM then!" Ashwin replied sitting on the chair. "Honestly, I can't be PM this year. That is sure!"

"Oh, *C'mon*! You are the most popular politician right now. I saw the predictions myself in the news. You are most likely to be our next PM according to the media. They can't be wrong?"

"That's the thing Arun!" Ashwin replied. "The reality is completely different from what is shown to the public," he said grimacing as his back hurt.

"Your back is hurting, eh?"

"A lot!" Ashwin said massaging his back with his hands to alleviate the pain and then added, "We need a majority for me to become PM. To get the majority, we need a miracle! It's not like I will bring a mammoth change after I will become PM, like I used to think earlier. I have been conditioned long enough to know that this change thing is all bullshit. It's impossible to bring any change with remittent internal opposition and outside negotiations. Honestly, I doubt I will have enough energy left for change after the continuous sycophancy of lawmakers, ass licking of industry moguls, un-altruistic international policies, and staged relationship struggles with some foreign countries. But if I will have control, whatever energy or time I will be left with, I will subliminally dedicate it to the betterment of the country. And this control is possible only if we have the majority."

"So you need a miracle?" Arun asked lighting another cigarette.

"Exactly!"

"But right now, India needs a leader like Ashwin Jamwal. We see hope in you."

"You will be disappointed," Ashwin replied sadly.

"Don't say that! You will win. You are better than all those motherfuckers combined."

"Well that's comforting. I am saying you will be disappointed even if I become the Prime Minister, which, in all likelihood, is not going to happen."

"Can I help?"

"Zero chance. Nobody can help." Ashwin sighed pulling out a cigarette.

"Then why hurt your back? If you are so sure, go home and sleep," Arun said angrily.

"How will you justify use of party funds to the investors? And if we don't campaign, we might end up losing our security! We may not form the government, but we will build the foundation for the state elections. Also, we don't want a humiliating defeat. If not the Prime Minister, I could become the opposition leader," he spoke off-handedly, much to Arun's irritation.

"Just to save your face? That's it?"

'That's it. And to become one devilish opposition leader."

"Stop joking!" Arun said, disturbed with the news and Ashwin's nonchalance. "You are frustrating me!" Arun flicked his cigarette and then added. "What help do you need? Jumping the law, connecting to a lawmaker, or stopping ballot rigging? I can help you in many more ways than you think.

"I know. Thank you. But we only need a miracle."

"Jesus resurrection type miracle?"

Ashwin laughed, "No US Presidential election type."

"I didn't get that!"

"In the US, some events happened just before the presidential election, forcing people to believe in the agenda of a party. Even those opposing them started believing in that particular party. In short, an event which can get you mass number of votes even from people who are against you. That's the miracle!"

"Can your party do something like that?" Arun asked. "Using your party's agenda of clean and neat politics?"

Ashwin nodded so he continued, "Plan a sting operation. Show the real face of corrupt politicians to the public."

"Sting operation is suicide. As of now, I have over hundreds of files on each politician. The thing is, even they have similar files on us. If we can go to media, so can they. The mudslinging will begin. It will become dirty as hell, for us as well!"

"Riots? What about polarization of votes?"

"Polarization is worse. In India, voters are already divided by urban, rural, literacy and technology. Then to top it all, there is the religion card, which further divides them into communities. And then it gets dirty for both the party and people. Besides, if the religion card is not played with utmost caution, the party can end up losing face forever. Why do you think nobody instigates a communal riot before elections?" Ashwin let out a sigh, feeling depressed with his insouciance towards miseries of communal violence. He crushed his cigarette. "I will be off in a while."

Arun was astonished, "I thought you would stay here tonight. We have made arrangements. Leave early in the morning."

"I know. Thanks! But I have to work on the rally."

"But that isn't until day after tomorrow."

"I know," Ashwin said uneasily, "and believe me, I want to stay. This is the closest thing to home that I have stayed in after months. I so want to be here, watch a movie, play a game on the PlayStation with you. Beat you, again!" He smiled and Arun rolled his eyes. "But I can't afford to, not now, when both Armugham and Inderji are absent."

"Is it true that Armugham considered you his son?" Arun asked

"Yes!" Ashwin said uneasily, "Param backed it up with evidence. Armugham was always protective about me like a father. He never told me that though!"

"That's sad," Arun said thinking. "Thank God nobody knows about your confrontation with him."

"Everybody knows about that!"

"What?"

"Except for the public! We had to pay the media pimp something around fifty lakhs every day so that the news about my confrontation and his subsequent heart attack does not reach the masses; that would reveal the dirty conflict in the party. We didn't want that!'

"Wow! I stopped listening after fifty lakhs!" Arun let out a whistle.

"That's nothing. Believe me!"

"So everybody knows, except for us?"

"The news was out before I could take Armugham to the hospital!" Ashwin said rubbing his hands on his pants to wipe the sweat. *Guilt.*

"Have your party members ever spoken to you about it?"

"Nobody said anything on my face, but I am sure they all are talking behind my back. I can't help it. I am at fault."

"Don't blame yourself, apparently all the evidences were against him," Arun said firmly.

"You remember I told you I saw truth in Armugham's eyes that day?"

Arun sighed, "I hoped you were wrong!"

"Why?"

"Because that means your enemy is very much alive."

"Oh? I never thought that way," Ashwin said leaning back and looking up at the sky.

"So please don't trust anyone...not even Raathi. Where is he, by the way?"

"He is unwell and is on some retreat. I don't know... some rejuvenation shit!"

"I don't like that guy."

"I trust Inderji!"

"Exactly. Don't trust anyone!" Arun said, and then added in irritation. "What's up there?"

"Nothing. Just looking at the sky; bright stars in the dark sky. Such a contrast. I love contrast! It makes a perfect blend. Complete opposites. That's why they can coexist. Two similar forces cannot function together; even though they have the same purpose, they cannot bring an act to fruition. Strong opposite forces, on the other hand, can. Similars repel, opposites attract. The yin and yang of life."

"Like us!" Arun laughed.

Ashwin looked at him, "Just like us."

"In our synergy, I am the better one, though."

"What? There is nothing such as 'better' in synergies."

"Whatever. I am the shaft, the protector…I am the better one. This is not synergy then," Arun said punching his fingers in the air to make his point.

"What? How childish!" Ashwin laughed.

"Still the better one!"

Ashwin was about to reply, when his phone buzzed. "Urrggh! Looks like it's time for me to go!" he said getting up and taking out the phone from his pocket.

Unknown number.

He slid over the screen and cleared his throat before saying, "Jamwal here," and then exclaimed, "Inderji? How are you? Where are you?"

Arun watched as Ashwin moved back to the railing. Ashwin looked confused. The call went a little over a minute.

"All is well?' Arun asked going towards him, "Who was that? Raathi?"

Ashwin nodded, a little lost. "That was strange."

"What did he say?"

"He said, don't worry you will be the Prime Minister this year, and I will ensure that. Then something like I will give you what I wanted to take from you!"

"What's that?"

"I don't know," Ashwin frowned.

"And how will *he* make you the PM?"

"Oh, he said he has something which will get the work done," Ashwin paused and then exclaimed, "Oh my God! Shit! The tapes!" he gripped Arun's hand in anxiety.

"What tapes?"

"The scandalous tapes I told you about. The sting operations."

"How did he get that?"

"I don't know…from my system? I just hope he doesn't turn those to the media."

"Call him. *Now!*" Arun urged.

Ashwin felt the sweat breaking on his forehead as he dialled the number. "The number is switched off!"

"Do you have some other number? Private...personal... call all the numbers!"

Ashwin did, and they were all switched off.

"I need to go now," he said starting for the door.

♌

Arun's phone vibrated. It was three a.m. and he couldn't go back to sleep. He was worried that, somebody had got access to Ashwin's private files. More than that, he was worried that Ashwin's assaulter was still alive. And above all, he was worried because he had asked Ashwin to message him about the status of the situation, but Ashwin has not messaged him yet. When his phone buzzed he almost pounced on it. It was Ashwin's text:

The system not accessed. Files have not been touched remotely or otherwise. But not 100% sure.

What the hell! He called Ashwin immediately.

"Then?" he asked.

"You awake?" Ashwin asked. His voice was hoarse with exhaustion.

"So what now?" Arun ignored his question.

"We can only hope he doesn't do anything like we have discussed."

"You guys took umm...measures?" Arun said consciously, to avoid blurting out anything controversial, just in case Ashwin's phone was being tapped.

"Yes!" Ashwin said almost forcing his words out. "Please go to sleep, because I will now. Don't worry!"

Arun went back to bed thinking. When Ashwin said 'Don't worry', how much would he have to pay the media pimp to ensure there was *nothing* to worry about. 'Fifty lakhs a day is nothing' had said.

"Some use of our hard-earned money!" Arun said bitterly.

INDER MOHAN RAATHI

I remember I was perspiring while furnishing the details to my banker, to finish a secure transaction. The reason for the nervousness was the amount of money getting transferred, and the number of things that were at stake. The amount had to go! Without fail.

When I founded the Nationalistic Party, I knew it would not be a smooth ride. I have worked for the Government of India for more than twenty-five years. I know things don't happen; you have to make them happen. I also know that corruption is the innate virtue of politics. It is dirty and to make politics appear clean, I have to sweep the dirt under the rug, and pay a heavy price to the person helping me do it. This clean politics image is costing me a bomb. As if that is not enough, there is always a gun on my back to make faster payments. People are impatient in this profession, because betrayal is very common.

Look at the irony of my life. In the process to have absolute control, I am being controlled! But then that's how it has been and always will be.

The banker left with the form and I waited. He said that the online transaction would take only a couple of hours. I mentally calculated the amount again, converting dollars into Indian rupees and realized party funds have reduced considerably. I'd have to knock some industrialist's doors again.

♋

It must have been around four when my phone rang. I was in my office alone, proofreading my speech. I absently disengaged phone from the cradle without removing my eyes from the paper.

The voice on the other end read out details of the transaction

500,000 US$	-	Prague
80,000 US$	-	Guangzhou
150,000 US$	-	Bonn
120, 000 US$	-	Brunei
800,000 US$	-	Zurich

"Correct?" he asked when he finished, and only then I realized that the call was not from the actual receiver of the money, but someone else. I got alarmed. How does he know the transaction details?

Damn the banker!

I cursed myself and wanted to disconnect the phone, but that would only affirm my involvement.

"I don't know what you are talking about," I said.

"You fucking well do, dammit!"

"Oh, I guess you have dialled the wrong number," I replied staying calm. The caller was male with a hoarse voice.

"I wish that too." He sighed. "Be on the line," he added putting me on hold, which meant he was reconfirming his details.

"Do you know who you are talking to?" I said the moment the line was active again. "You may have dialled the wrong number," I wanted to confuse him. "But what you gave me were extraordinary numbers," I kept talking even though I wasn't sure if the caller was listening. "What are these numbers?"

"Doesn't matter," the voice spoke, "I want you to pull the curtain of the window overlooking Gandhi Street. If you have a cordless, take it with you or else run back and give me an update."

"What if I don't do that?" I asked firmly, annoyed at the order.

"Oh! You wouldn't."

"Do you know whom you are talking to?" I asked authoritatively.

"A corrupt politician, salivating for power," he replied flatly.

"Then you should know that I can find you and get you killed!" I said under my breath.

The voice laughed, and that made me nervous.

"How will you find me?" He laughed again. "This call is already way over ten minutes and I am going to talk more. Trace the call, will you? But you won't! You can't!"

I know how much I hated that aplomb. The caller was good; he knows I have a lot to lose. Even if an iota of information leaked, I'd be done for, forever!

"There is a reason why I asked you to move over to the window. Please do that!" The voice stressed. "We both are busy people. We must not waste time."

I found it legit. I moved to the window and saw nothing unusual, I told him that.

"What were you expecting, a loaded bomber or something?" he mocked and I hated him more. I started thinking of ways to outsmart him, but soon realized that this man had got transaction details from one of the most secure financial institutions. He must be really smart. I was thinking and didn't realize that I had been ignoring the caller till I heard him cry out, "Mother fucking fool!"

"What?"

"I said you are a fool."

"Is it? We will find out. I know how you got these details," I said infuriated. "Sharma gave them to you!"

"The banker? Oh no. He is way too loyal to you for my liking! Besides, he doesn't have details to this precision. You filled some of the details yourself as a security measure! So yes, you are a fool and we are wasting time."

The moment I heard that the details were not given by the banker, I realized he must have intercepted the online transaction remotely. I didn't know whether to be appalled or amazed by this man's capability.

"I can see Gandhi Road," I replied.

"Great! Can you spot a man in an orange shirt outside the Bata Showroom?"

I spotted him almost immediately. He was a skinny man in his twenties wearing an orange shirt, brown pants and cheap dark sunglasses.

"I see him. Is he a gunner?" I asked confused.

"For you? No. That's my life security. The brown envelope that he is holding has all the transaction details I just read out. And to confirm that he is my man, please see him respond about now." The caller did not speak for a few seconds, but the man stirred; he took out a phone from his pocket and looked across, towards my window. My stomach churned. This man is for real!

"You can wave to him if you want," the caller said jokingly. "He is not harmful, but if you ever think of tracing the call and harming me in any way, this man will send the details to the right person. Oh! Did I tell you there are many more copies?"

"What do you want?" I said moving away from the window.

"Now we are talking! When you will know of my demand—"

"Money?" I interrupted.

"No!"

"Party ticket?"

"What? No!"

"A favour from the government?"

"Shut up, you time wasting fool!" he said angrily. "Instead of throwing baseless options, you could just listen to me!"

I could have actually listened to him, but I had to show that I had been in this game for a long time and I knew how it is played. Well, I was wrong. I was dumbfounded when I heard his demand.

He wanted me to convince a newly-appointed DC to join my party. *What?*

"Who are you?" I asked.

"I am a player, just like you. Just playing bigger games of power and politics."

"I am not playing any game."

"Hell, you are! More than I can imagine."

"Who is this Ashwin Jamwal? And why are you pushing him into politics?" I asked finally.

"He is just a random guy. Let's say his name came out in the lottery. I am doing my own sets of experiments before my final move. Ashwin is my guinea pig."

"What if I say no?"

"Let's not go into the loop again."

"What will you get from this?" I felt as if I was talking to a maniac.

"That time will tell," he sighed and then added, "I am giving you three years to get Ashwin to join your party; three years and nothing more."

"Three years? Not now?"

"Can you do it now? Do it!"

He challenged me and I thought about the impracticality of the operation. The caller was intelligent and wise. I would rather have this man in the party than some random guys he suggested.

I learned about Ashwin Jamwal who turned out to be an honest DC in Rajasthan; so honest that he had had three or four transfers in just two years. I cursed my unknown caller! And I understood exactly why he had given me a period of three years. You cannot brainwash an idealist with the snap of your fingers. It takes time.

Since the Nationalistic Party started in Rajasthan, I had no trouble approaching Ashwin. I met him in the Jhalwar district office regarding a mass rally. He looked familiar and before I could say anything in this regard, he told me that I had asked him to join politics.

"Well, will you?" I asked him. He shook his head. Darn!

I realized that Ashwin was a crushed soul. He was painfully honest and upright; such moral beings do not survive in politics. Only if I had means to contact my unknown caller, I would have told him that Ashwin is not fit for the job. Maybe he could find someone else. I had already started conditioning another young professional, Param. Then one day I heard some news about Ashwin, which threw me off-guard. I heard he was adopting unlawful measures to do the right things! Ashwin directly locked horns with Rangbahadur Singh, the single most powerful man in that area. Singh's ego was hurt with the defeat and he was planning to eliminate Ashwin, but then I took charge and started controlling the events around him. I wanted to give Ashwin confidence in adopting illicit means. So I reached out to the man, who is a master in such simulation – Ashok Kumar Nandi.

For more than two years, we ensured that Ashwin's operations were successful. He was good and thorough, but he made a lot of enemies. Had it not been for Nandi, either his enemies would have killed him or brought him back on track by torturing his family.

I remember we all were biting our nails while staging the Lohia incident. We wanted everything to happen perfectly. The slightest mistake could send our efforts down the drain. On top of everything, Nandi put a bomb in my head by saying, "What if he commits suicide?" His suicide would be my end. We had to ensure that Ashwin didn't take such a step, so we looped in his most loyal informer Suraj.

Suraj convinced Ashwin to resign. I did the rest of the work and Ashwin joined us two weeks after he resigned from his post in Udaipur.

I did not care about Ashwin after he joined the party. I was busy making plans for our first general assembly elections. It was only after the campaigns were over that I realized the true potential of Ashwin Jamwal. That young man had everything you need to make a good politician. Dishonesty? That would come with time.

I can't say I have worked on Ashwin, because I haven't! The nature of the job is such that it will mould you in its shape before you know it. In five years, Ashwin emerged as one of the strongest party members. He was hardworking, passionate and resourceful. I swear to God when I nominated him as the PM candidate, it was only because I didn't have a better option. Ashwin had immense popularity on the social media. The young generation loved the idea of an ever so charming politician, who was honest, compassionate and humorously direct. And girls? They loved his looks. If only all these people would go out and vote, we'd win by a majority! Besides the social media, the analysis from R&A agencies also gave similar results – India needs a goal-oriented leader who is young and enthusiastic, someone with whom a majority of people can relate to. Of all the parties, only we had one such candidate – Ashwin! So, then, I didn't have a choice.

I must have slapped myself a hundred times later.

I should have stopped after nominating Ashwin as the PM candidate. But then I had to handover the president-ship to him only to please the designation hungry lot, for whom designation signifies stature. While the young crowd welcomed the politician in large aviator sunglasses, it was hard to appease the other half, which was appalled by the sunglasses and hoodie. Not just that, Ashwin had never contested from any constituency. They would never take him seriously, until and unless there was a designation attached to his name, so I gave up mine!

It all seems so stupid now.

Oh how I repent empowering Ashwin! Ever heard of the old adage – putting your foot on an axe? Well here I put my neck on it! Ashwin Jamwal started becoming more powerful and before I knew it, he surpassed the man who made him what he is – I.M. Raathi!

In less than one year, the Nationalistic Party became more like the Jamwal Party. My name was getting faded. I never wanted to promote myself, because then I would have absolute control and nobody to answer to. But then, I only wanted my name to be out of the radar, not me as an individual. Sadly the latter began happening, and I just couldn't take it.

I was the one who had formed the Nationalistic Party. I was the one who had moved the nation with provoking speeches, and brought the Nationalistic Party to the national political arena. I made Nationalistic Party. Me!

Besides I had commitments. The investors are no fools; they would not fill my pocket if they didn't see money flowing into theirs. I promised them that! But could I do it now? That bloody Ashwin took that power from me. My neck was under the guillotine, whose blades were sliding down slowly.

Now that the strings had been cut, the puppet was useless for the puppeteer and I decided to eliminate Ashwin.

Murugan Swamy was Armugham's source. We have used Swamy for activities which we can't do in broad daylight. Initially, we approached Murugan through Armugham. Gradually I started establishing contact with him directly, without intimating Armugham. Once I had pulled Swamy out of a deep mess; the unspoken obligations were understood, I approached him to carry out Ashwin's assassination.

We made all the plans. The assassin was brought in and he began moving with us obtrusively. He had been ordered to occasionally talk to Armugham, whenever he was out in the open. With everything planned, all we needed was an opportunity. The wait was long, or it felt so, because I had to pay the assassin and his aides every day for keeping an eye on us and waiting for the signal – wiping my glasses thrice and putting them back on.

That day when Ashwin went out from the hotel suite, I moved to the balcony for fresh air. I saw the assassin's informer strolling idly by the pool. He was occasionally looking up. I gave the signal.

My heart was beating fast, so I chose a secluded place in the corner, buried myself in my laptop and refused to be disturbed for some time. I don't know for how long I sat there pretending to work. Finally I heard the news about the ambush.

But wait! This is not what I wanted to hear!

"Tea shop boy has come for help!"

What? Tea shop boy? They went outside? The assassin shot them outside? Not in the garden? But then we never gave such instructions to him. These cold-hearted assassins are like robots. You have to feed in every detail to get your desired output.

Damn!

I pretended to fall sick. Just before lying on the couch I asked weakly, "Did you get that ruthless man?" The answer was negative, but the tea shop boy may have seen him. The assassin had to be eliminated.

After sometime I called Murugan Swamy for a meeting in a Dubai hotel. He agreed. He was very embarrassed to have failed in his first attempt, which usually didn't happen. He was ready for the second phase of execution. This time, I didn't even have to pay him as much. He told me he had the assassin killed.

We kept talking and discussing the next steps for almost two hours. He promised he would assign the job to a better assassin the next time. He promised he would ensure that there would be no mistake the next time. He was making plans and I was getting jittery. I did not have much time with me.

Finally I decided to finish the conversation, so I got up and fired point blank.

Murugan was thrown from the couch with the impact of the first bullet which hit his left shoulder. His right hand instinctively reached for the weapon tucked under his shirt, but before he could pull out a gun, I fired twice more, hitting his vital organs this time. Once his body went limp, I checked for the pulse. There wasn't any. I fired again on his forehead just to be sure.

Murugan Swamy has arranged for this highly secretive meeting and nobody knew that I had come to meet him. He must have thought I was harmless for he didn't have security. He must have thought I couldn't even slap him, let alone kill him. He was wrong. He must have thought I did not blame him for the failure. He was wrong again. As much as I wanted to eliminate all the evidence, I was vindictive too.

I flew home and began planning and strategizing my next step. I was so drowned in my pursuit of control that I actually forgot that all this had begun with a phone call, ten years back!

I remember it now. Too late.

♞

The morning weather of Kasauli can instil romance even in stone. The soft morning breeze that touched Raathi's face had an earthen smell to it. Raathi was standing in the balcony, savouring the morning freshness before turning back and moving inside a nondescript room.

Inside, he read the script twice: once while looking at the paper, then without it. The man standing on his left acknowledged the content, before switching on the small speaker phone.

A voice from the phone filled the room. There was a little disturbance in the line, but the message was clear.

"Ready are we?" asked the voice.

"Yes!" said the man and Raathi together.

"Please start," said the voice. Raathi knew what he was supposed to do. He opened his laptop and started talking.

♌

When Ashwin heard the news, he jolted up so suddenly that it gave him a minor neck spasm. It had been days since he had spoken to Raathi in Bhopal. He made arrangements to ensure that nothing from Raathi should reach the press. But Ashwin forgot the expanse of digital media. The thing with digital media is that it's uncontrollable. Raathi had uploaded a video on hundreds of different websites which had gone viral in less than twenty minutes, before Ashwin's technology team could pull it out.

"A new website with the video is surfacing every second!" said the IT in-charge, in defence. Ashwin shushed him as he opened the laptop and played the video.

Raathi appeared to be sitting on a heavy chair; there was nothing behind him except for a black curtain. He looked fresh and healthy, but his eyes were cold and devoid of emotions. He cleared his throat and began,

"I always wanted to see India as corruption free country. I have worked for the government, and as a diplomat I have travelled all across the globe, representing the nation for twenty-five years. While I am proud to be an Indian, I feel small when I compare our country with others."

Ashwin had to turn away from the screen as his phone kept on buzzing. He silenced it and turned back.

"We stand nowhere. Be it infrastructure, governance, technology, anything. We are far behind even from our Asian counterparts! We have envisioned 2020, but are we on track? No. Everything is on paper; nothing comes to ground. And nothing will ever happen if we keep on electing this corrupt leech like government. But we are so myopic in our approach…we all think of our present gains and comforts and ignore future needs. By the looks of the way things are going, believe me, very soon our country will be in shambles. I know you find it hard to believe, but history has many prosperous nations turning to rubble because of corruption at the top. It's sad. I can see my country turning into one such nation.

"I have seen deaths and miseries of our children and I have also seen the guys on top eating their fill that very moment; eating out of a famished child's plate. That's how gluttonous these pigs are!

"I just wanted to change that. God knows I tried! I tried hard. My party slogged day and night just to make you understand the importance of a clean government. But you all are so reluctant, blinded by false promises and baseless commitments. You all are so divided by region, religion, community, caste, sex, education and what not. India can never think together or act together. But then we tried, because at this juncture a clean government becomes as important as oxygen to breathe.

"We tried and you never listened. We still tried and tried harder, but failed! We all failed because you refused to rationalize. They squandered all your hard-earned money and gave you nothing. They made mountains of molehills and you started believing in an illusion. You never questioned why you don't have something as basic as security?

"Have you really stopped caring? Don't you think it's high time to demand services? Don't you want better roads, hospitals, schools? Have you all given up? Accepted this as the only way of life? Inflation has increased, GDP has come down, women are not safe, education is becoming costlier, yet you can't speak. You are scared and you are okay with it. It pains me! I get frustrated, how do I make all of you see?

"Well, I for one, who started the movement to bring in clean politics, cannot see you remain delusional any more. It pains me to see you struggling every day. Whether you choose it or not, you do not deserve such a life. But then you have stopped rationalizing and that hurts me more. I can't see it any longer.

"I, Inder Mohan Raathi, founder of the Nationalistic Party and believer of a clean government leave, you all to your destiny, with a hope that my sacrifice opens your eyes and makes you realize your priorities. I wish you well. Jai Hind…"

Raathi then took out a gun from his left, put it on his right temple and pressed the trigger. Blood splashed all over. A patch masked a part of the screen. Ashwin noticed a small lump of his brain and gagged.

Raathi had died for a reason.

Ω

A month later, thirty-nine-year-old Ashwin Jamwal was sworn in as Prime Minister. The Nationalistic Party won the Assembly elections with a majority, breaking all the previous records.

♌

Hades looked at the newspaper; beneath a big skybus advertisement was the headline 'Ashwin Jamwal is new Prime Minister of India'. He smiled.

"First phase is over, first step is taken," he said to himself.

Part-II

Thou art the path of holy order, the shadow of the gods, the name of immortality; thou art truth

—Yajur Veda, Taittiriya Samhita, Khand VII 1.20

A speedboat was going at the speed of twenty knots on the Andaman Sea. The old boatman was miffed with his passengers: two black men, two white men and one Thai. The old man was angry because he had been instructed to take the boat almost a hundred kilometres away from the island. They had been circling around for more than twenty minutes now, and he hadn't got any instructions. He was angry because the passengers were all talking to each other very quietly, in English, and he couldn't understand a thing. It was a hot afternoon and he was getting restless.

After almost forty-five minutes, he was given instructions to slow down the speed of his boat and wait for another vessel which was bringing a passenger. The other boat came and left almost immediately. The old man looked behind as the new passenger settled on his boat. He must be very athletic because in spite of the lurching and shifting of the wooden plank which acted as bridge between two vessels, this man lunged into his boat effortlessly.

"Pi! Langan!" the old man heard the Thai man's voice. He started the engine; this was his command to keep the boat in motion at a constant speed of twenty knots.

♌

Zahan jumped into the boat carrying an old-styled brown suitcase. He was representing his boss, Hades, in another secret ammunition meeting. The men on the boat worked for Juan Carlos Moreno who claimed to own one of the most diversified illegal ammunition supplies in the world.

Zahan looked at his fellow passengers; he knew most of them. The black guys were the 'Kimetto brothers'. The elder one, Timonthy Kimetto was shorter than his younger brother Nirjye. Then there was the Russian, Gustov, with thick blond hair; he had met the stout academic man before, but he didn't remember his name. He had never met the Thai.

Zahan put the suitcase on the floor and sat between the Kimetto brothers.

"We have done our part, now you will take from here. I will connect you guys with Kuruserv tomorrow; you will intercept him in a week's time in the Caribbean. I will be a part of your first call, and then from there, you have to take the ownership. I will get back on the scene once the supply is made. Day after tomorrow, you will meet a guy name David Muniz. He will be your contact till further information," Zahan pulled out a business card and gave it to Timonthy. He then took out a small USB dongle-like device. "This is your passcode to reach Muniz," he said giving that device to Timonthy, "It's deactivated right now, you will be informed when it's activated." He paused as he noticed a frown on Timonthy's face. "Any problem?"

"I know this man. He is in software." Timonthy said squinting at the card.

"He is an entrepreneur. What's the problem?" asked Zahan.

"Well…Does he have…will he be of any use?"

"He has enough funds for us, what more do we require?" Zahan shrugged.

"What I mean to say is – this man is suit and tie businessman with a card and all. There are fair chances of scrutiny of his funds," Tim said.

"Yes, I agree! None of us have flashy business cards, nor do we move around in public meetings. Just because he has funds, doesn't make him suitable for the job and besides people like him succumb easily to pressure," Nirjye spoke shifting a little farther from Zahan.

"Yeah, yeah! You could be right, but he is the man for the job. That's what I have been told and that's how it will be."

"So you agree with us?" Nirjye asked.

"Yeah, you could be right, but then I don't ask questions."

"Don't you think you should?" Nirjye asked.

"I don't get paid to ask questions or answer any," Zahan said turning to look at Nirjye.

"Now, now!" Nirjye said. "I just asked because I thought we have developed a rapport."

"It's only a professional association," Zahan corrected him.

"Yes, yes, only a professional association!" Nirjye said though his ego was hurt by Zahan's effrontery. "But of all the three or four Hades' employees we have met—"

"There must be more. Ten perhaps," Zahan interrupted.

"More? Too many faces, only a few I remember," Nirjye said irritated with the interruption. "You are our favourite! You are not raw, you are very civil, you have class, a flair...what's that word?" Nirjye clicked his tongue.

"Panache?"

"Umm...What does it mean?" Nirjye asked embarrassed at his poor knowledge of English.

"The class... flair? What do you want?" Zahan asked flatly.

"I don't want anything!" Nirjye replied defensively. "I look at you and I am like...this is the man who is smart, takes decisions, but brother, does he ask questions? Like me?"

"I take orders."

"I don't believe you. Over ten years and you have never asked why or what?" Tim asked in astonishment.

"Your boss doesn't ask Hades any questions either. That's how it is!" Zahan said irritated.

"My boss doesn't need to know!"

"Yeah right! Hades controls your boss. He knows where you are, what you are, and who you are. Juan doesn't know anything about Hades and its killing him, so he asked you to inquire," he said looking at Nirye's shocked face. "Sorry to disappoint you. I don't know anything, except that may be because of *this* your boss might be thrown out of the deal."

"We shall see," Timonthy replied standing up.

Before Zahan could react, Gustov and Nirjye pinned him down. Timonthy hit him so hard on his face that he fell onto his left, and blood trickled down from his nose. Zahan's reflexes urged him to wipe the blood and estimate the damage, but as he moved, they tightened the grip.

"Now tell me what do you know about your boss or I will give you a death you cannot even dream of."

"Believe me, I have seen death. I have felt its pain many times. I don't fear it. There have been times I longed for it," Zahan said swaying unsteadily. Timonthy knew that Zahan was not afraid of death. Besides, his death would not get him any answer. He motioned his eyes to the stout man and he jumped into action. The stout man opened a small bag and took out a bottle and syringe. Zahan's eyes widened and he began throwing his feet. The interpreter and Timonthy grasped his legs tightly, making him immobile. The stout man gripped his right arm and injected. Zahan cried not so much in pain as much in helplessness. He knew he was getting injected with psychological drugs. The bottle contained a cocktail of psychological chemicals including sodium thiopental – the truth serum.

Zahan struggled ferociously under captivity. He was beginning to feel pain in his chest. Then after a few seconds, all the sensations vanished. The men slowly removed their hands as Zahan's eyes turned inwards. His body grew limp. Gustov sat beside him and held him straight.

"What's your name?" Timonthy asked.

"Za-ahn," Zahan replied, twisting and turning his head. "Za-ahn Mubaraq Al-uidden."

Tim noticed his accent wasn't British anymore, it was Middle Eastern. The chemicals worked!

"Who do you work for?"

"Had...Hades!"

"Damn! What's his real name?" Timonthy shouted.

"Hades," Zahan replied his head swaying. Gustov jerked him to sit up straight again.

"You son of a bitch! What's his real name?"

"H-a-d-es," came the reply, much to Timonthy's irritation.

"What does he do?" Timonthy changed his question. The thing with these chemicals is that you have to ask the right questions to get the desired answers.

"Business...ammunition business."

"And energy?"

"Oil and energy reserve," Zahan replied feebly.

"Who is he?" Timonthy asked and got 'Hades' again. He knew he had to feed the right command, so he asked again.

"How do you meet him for orders?"

"I... never...met him...Ahhh," Zahan replied in pain.

"What?" Nirjye and Timonthy cried in unison. Ten years as a loyalist and Zahan never met Hades?

"How do you get orders?" Timonthy asked again, trying hard to maintain his cool.

"Phones, voices...different voices... female...male...different people..."

Different people? Hades is not one man? Did he say female? Timonthy was shocked.

"Is he one man?" he asked pushing Zahan to sit up straight.

"I don't know."

"What the fuck!" Timonthy hit his fist on the seat in frustration. How can Zahan work for someone so insulated? Money? Why had he never asked any questions? Timonthy was getting restless.

"Where does he live?" he asked again. He didn't want to go to his boss empty handed.

"So many places…Urrgghhh," Zahan said clutching his abdomen.

"How does he control? Who all are behind him? Where is he accessible?" In anxiety, Timothy darted three questions together. It was a mistake because under the influence of the chemicals, the already jumbled up brain could get confused further. Timothy also knew that the chemical is would be of no use now. The questions were more directed towards himself than Zahan.

"I…voices…" Zahan couldn't finish as he flinched and vomited on Gustov's pants.

"Ublyudok!" Gustov cursed before getting up. Zahan, now without support, fell on the floor unconscious.

"Shit! Fuck!" Timonthy said kicking the bench in frustration. He recalled the conversation, and then whispered to his brother.

"Ammunition business, eh? Look at this thing," he said pointing at Zahan. "He kept saying ammunition business, bloody bastard! He and his boss are the biggest pimps of the world and this man is talking as if he is a fucking CEO or something."

Nirjye sensed frustration in his brother's voice. They had nothing to give to their boss today. Its repercussions could be life threatening. He looked at his watch. It was half past five and they had to be terra firma by eight. They should head back. He waved at the interpreter who nodded and got up immediately to give instructions to the boatman.

"When will he wake up?" Nirjye asked the stout man.

"In an hour or so."

They were supposed to send Zahan back on the boat by seven. "Will he be hostile?" he asked anxiously.

"Not for three days ! He will suffer from temporary amnesia. He will not even remember what happened. His mind will be too numb to carry out any fast reflexes for three days!" He looked at Zahan then asked Nirjye. "What will you do to him?"

"As planned, send him off on his boat at seven."

"That was when he was active and kicking! Not like this," the stout man said poking Zahan. "What will you say happened?"

"We will say he is sea sick or something." Nirjye replied irritated.

"Why not kill him?"

"Did you not hear him? The passcode is not activated and can only be activated by him. If he is dead, all our supplies will get stuck. That's his security. Besides, he is top guy for Hades! We cannot kill him!" Nirjye looked at his brother, who was standing at the edge of the boat staring aimlessly at the water.

♌

Juan Carlos Moreno stared at the poor quality video. The action on the boat was getting relayed live on his monitor.

Who is your boss?

Hades

He knew that! All the efforts had gone waste. His best men had failed. He was so shocked that he ignored the voice on his phone for a long time. The voice which gave him the link to watch the live action on that boat.

Hades

"You shouldn't have done that!" Hades said firmly.

"I did nothing!" replied Juan after he heard Hades' voice again. "Those Kimetto brothers are big in business too! They have minds of their own," he replied, his voice trembling.

"Sure they do!" Just like Zahan, Hades laughed. "People like them have their mind conditioned such that no amount of drug or pain can bring out any information that they are not supposed to share. It's like make believe – your illusion becomes your reality! For such people, the order from the top is the only reality. They are like robots. They can only read instructions and act upon them!"

"Your people are like that. Not mine!" Moreno emphasized.

"Then re-breed your lot! It's not good to be responsible for the death of a man with a working brain. A robot, on the other hand, can die and there is no regret."

♌

The boat was moving steadily. It was almost six. If the boatman maintained the same speed, the interception with the other vessel would happen at the designated time. The interception point was still far. There was no boat or land in sight. Only water. The passengers on the boat were sitting quietly. Zahan too had regained his consciousness. His body was still weak and even a small lurch could throw him off.

The old boatman wiped the sweat off his forehead. He opened a compartment near the wheel, drank some water, and then took out a small gun hidden behind several big water bottles. He got up unsteadily and turned to face his passengers. Within a minute all the men were on the floor, dead; all except Zahan. Zahan was still sitting idly. His eyes lacked any alertness whatsoever. The old man quickly checked on each passenger to reconfirm their deaths. Then he crouched and pulled out two diving gears which were kept under the bench. He checked the oxygen level in the tank and helped Zahan to get in one before wearing his own. He moved quickly and opened the brown suitcase which Zahan has brought. There were only documents. He emptied the contents of the suitcase and cautiously sliced the stitches of the bottom fabric, revealing a small watch like machine. He took out one blue wire from his pocket and removed the insulating plastic layer to get an inch of copper wire at each end. He connected the wire with the machine completing a circuit.

He took Zahan to the edge of the boat, put on the snorkel and jumped into water with him.

Half an hour later, the bomb in the boat exploded and within a few minutes, the entire boat sank.

$\unicode{x265E}$

Ashwin was hurriedly getting down the stairs to reach his designated seat. He was in Shanghai to attend the First International Industry Conference. His bodyguards had circled him and his assistant was speaking continuously, updating him on the schedule of the conference. A beautiful blonde was ushering them to their seats. There was something very pleasant about that woman, which made his entire entourage worthwhile. Ashwin thought he would speak to her later.

Engulfed in his own existence, Ashwin felt somebody call out his name. He stopped abruptly and turned left to look at the source of the voice. He must have overheard the organizers. He didn't know and didn't bother, because as he turned left he saw her sitting on one of the seats designated for the press. She wasn't looking at him. In fact, she was looking straight at the dais, but then as if pulled by some external force, she looked at his direction. Their eyes met for a second and then the black suited bodyguard blocked their line of vision.

Ashwin paralysed momentarily before being shoved forward. It all happened in a few seconds and in those few seconds he saw the face he had never forgotten.

Adya's.

Ashwin sat quietly at his designated spot. The conference had started and the speakers from various countries were taking the dais one by one to discuss their agenda. At one time, Ashwin had a feeling to just turn and look towards Adya. See her again.

The Vietnamese speaker was saying something in accented

English and it was difficult to understand. Ashwin knew he would get the complete transcript of the speech, so he did not bother to listen to him. He didn't want to hear anyone. His mind was not thinking straight. He had seen her! After fourteen years or so. He felt a pain in his chest as all the memories avalanched.

Ashwin got up from the chair and moved to the window restlessly. After the conference, he met diplomats from France and the UK. He then had discussions with his team about his speech which was due the next day. He wrapped everything before 8:30 p.m. because he had scheduled dinner with Adya. She had said she'd be there by 9:00 p.m.

It was past 9.30. and there was no sign of her.

Ashwin looked outside the window. Shanghai is a beautiful city, well developed. He saw that all the buildings were illuminated with neon lights. The animated billboards further added to the colour and festivity. Come to think of it, till 1980 Shanghai was nothing but a fishermen's village and by the end of the nineties, it was established as one of the best economic centres in the world. Ashwin mentally compared the tallest building in India with the skyscraper in front of him and was immediately filled with self-contempt. The tallest building in India was dwarfed by a random skyscraper in Shanghai. Ashwin established the analogy, the difference in height of the skyscrapers signifies his contribution to the country, or rather the lack of it. He felt guilty. He had been sitting on the Prime Minister's chair for six years. Winning with a majority the second time in a row. Indian people saw him as a messiah for change. They believed him, as they found his contributions mammoth. In truth, his contributions were nothing compared to what they should have been.

Ashwin looked at his watch as his stomach rumbled. It was close to ten and he was hungry. The hunger stimulated anger and frustration as he thought of Adya.

She left just like that fourteen years ago. Now she is doing it again. As though she gets pleasure in giving me pain. Leaving me clueless, waiting for her. And I have been blamed for being self-centred!

Ashwin thought and immediately felt silly. Adya was not self-centred. Adya would never think of hurting him. Then why the delay? Especially when all his staff knew about the meeting? Ashwin thought and the first thing that came to his mind was marriage. She must be married now. A woman is always answerable to her family, her husband especially. To tell her husband that she'd be going for dinner with the Indian Prime Minister would have raised eyebrows and if at all the husband knew about their relationship, she would have a lot of explaining to do.

Ashwin felt strange at the thought of seeing Adya with another man. He crossed the room and reached for the intercom kept on the bedside table. He would call off the meeting, he thought. Why create unnecessary ripples in someone's life? There was no point in digging up the past. Not after fourteen years. He dialled the extension and before the operator could respond, he heard a soft knock on the door.

"Come in," Ashwin called out and the chief security walked in followed by two guards, who ushered Adya in.

Ashwin let out a sigh of relief as he saw her. His brows straightened and a natural smile came on his face. All confusion was gone. He was delighted to see her again.

"Sir, let us know if you need anything," the security chief said before leaving.

Adya watched them leave and spoke, "I am sorry I am late." She didn't sound apologetic at all.

"I thought you would never come!" Ashwin said cheerfully, sitting on the bed. "Please sit," he motioned to her.

"Had to acknowledge the request from the Indian Prime Minister!" she replied dryly. Ashwin looked at her. She was dressed formally, as if she had come for a business meeting. He was dressed in loose pants and a sweatshirt. Her face exhibited no emotions, but her eyes showed compassion.

Adya noticed him looking at her eyes, and as if to hide any feeling whatsoever, she lowered them instantly and began walking towards the bed.

Ashwin watched her in silence, as she struggled to drag a leather armchair over the heavy carpet. He understood what it meant. He didn't like it, but he had to accept it. There was a distance between them. The gap created in the last fourteen years could not be filled in a moment.

"You had dinner?" he asked.

"Nope. I was invited for one!" she replied coldly.

"But you were late, I thought…Never mind. I will order the food."

"May I know the purpose of the meeting, sir?" she asked, her voice still cold, which irritated the hell out of him. He wanted to scream at her for her indifference. She could at least try. He was trying! But then for Ashwin, the distance between them was only physical. He couldn't say that for Adya. She could be emotionally detached to him.

"The purpose?" Ashwin said wearily stretching his legs. "It was purely personal, unless you want otherwise, then I am ready for a professional meeting as well. No issues," he said looking at the ceiling.

"Thank you, sir. Should I call in my assistant? We can do a quick Q&A," she spoke sombrely looking at Ashwin. "Do we need a formal consent to quote you?"

"Maybe, yes."

"I will get that arranged. I will call my assistant."

Ashwin propped himself on his elbow and looked at her. She wasn't joking.

"Can all this wait till after dinner? I wanted to do it quietly, for once," he asked irritably.

"Yes sir. I will just make a call and ask him to prep."

Ashwin let out a sigh and fell back on the bed in frustration. Adya added quickly, "I won't call him now."

"Thank you. Besides it is a special meal for two people only."

"Oh!"

"It's *makkey ki roti* and *sarson ka saag* – homemade style."

"Oh!" A smile automatically appeared on Adya's face. She hoped Ashwin hadn't seen it. He did not. But he heard it – that slight change in tone. A childlike excitement. Makkey ki roti was her favourite.

Ashwin sat up straight, feeling fresh again, "And there are more surprises!" he added.

Adya has always been a foodie.

"And guessing by what you have just told me, I know exactly what we are going to have for dinner," Adya said, her lips trembling as she tried to hold back her smile.

"Tell me," Ashwin said smiling and sitting up.

"Well let's see...rogan josh, biriyani for sure, naan, of course! Kababs and some tikkas perhaps for starters...a shawarma roll? It isn't rocket science," Adya said beaming.

Ashwin laughed. "Actually, there are *no* surprises! Makkey ki roti it is! Don't you think the other stuff would be too much for dinner?"

"Oh I thought you ordered a kingly meal for me with all my favourite dishes!"

"To have all your favourite dishes, *in this hotel*, could negatively impact the Indian economy!"

Adya burst into laughter; her laugh deep, just as it used to be. It pierced straight to his heart. He felt alive. *Distance shortens. Soon there will be none.*

They ate in silence, mostly because they both went back in time. Their minds were too ecstatic to mix the present with the past. Another reason for the silence was the good food; it complemented their memories.

"You look different," Ashwin said as he finished his plate. Adya was still eating.

"I am a different person now," she replied. She was finishing the food with her hands, just like the earlier days. Ashwin smiled to himself – in what way princess?

"You and I, both!" Ashwin said looking at her plate.

"How am I different? Have I put on weight?" she asked pushing away her plate.

"Nope. Just the chubbiness which comes with age," Ashwin said getting up and moving over to the heavy wooden table where the alcohol was kept.

"But I wasn't talking about that. Your attire, you were not comfortable in formals at all. I remember you refused to wear formals at your workplace and created a lot of fuss. Your point was how can you work if you are not comfortable. You remember that? You gave your HR guy such a hard time."

"Yeah! Now I advocate wearing formals!" Adya replied moving over to the window.

"Have I changed?" Ashwin asked but Adya did not reply and kept looking outside the window.

Ashwin stood there in silence for some time and then poured himself a drink. Adya must have heard the clinking of the ice, because she turned immediately to face him.

"Vodka?" Ashwin asked, "Or has that changed as well?" he added acidly.

She nodded. "With orange juice."

"I have to check," Ashwin said opening the mini-bar. "If not, we could still get some for you."

"Privileges!"

"Yeah! The same kind that you have. It's called room service!" Ashwin said getting up with a can of orange juice in his hand.

Before they could start drinking, the intercom rang. It was close to eleven, so Ashwin listened for a few seconds and disconnected the call.

"Anything urgent?" Adya asked.

"Sort of. It will take only five minutes, max. Let's go to another room," he said touching Adya's shoulder and gently taking her to an adjoining room. "That room was rather personal!"

"How many rooms do you have in your suite?"

Ashwin ignored her question and took his place on a couch in a room which looked like an office area. Just as Adya sat down, a very beautiful girl in an indigo shift dress came in. Adya watched as the girl handed some papers to Ashwin and moved around the couch to stand behind him. While Ashwin was reading the content of the paper, she noticed the girl was leaning a bit more than required, revealing her cleavage. Some of her black hair was falling on Ashwin's shoulder and Adya could swear that more than once she saw that girl turning over to face Ashwin, her lips only millimetres away from his face. To her surprise, Ashwin did not retract, even once! In fact, he laughed softly on a number of occasions referring to the content on the paper. Did he not mind those obvious moves by that girl? She also felt the pain of a thousand needles on her neck and chest. Jealousy.

She looked away. She was uncomfortable. Ashwin had not introduced her to this girl. Five minutes he had said. It had been more than twenty. Adya drank her vodka in one gulp out of frustration. She was thinking of going back to her room, when Ashwin got up and stretched. The meeting was over.

"I am really sorry!" he said as the girl left.

"Five minutes?"

"I am *really* sorry!" Ashwin said picking up his empty glass and starting for the bed room. "How long did I take?"

"Over thirty minutes!"

Ashwin let out a soft whistle adding to Adya's irritation.

"Your secretary is rather pretty," Adya said, following him to the bedroom.

"Secretary?" He laughed softly. "Krupa is not my secretary! She handles PR," he replied making his drink. "You want one?"

"I could have one, *right now!*" Adya said.

"A rather charming PR girl you have," Adya said taking her drink from Ashwin. "So, have you appointed her intentionally or is it just luck?" she added and Ashwin laughed.

"Her? She is a bachchi! But she is good at her work," he said sitting on the bed.

"She was totally hitting on you!"

"What? No way!" Ashwin tried to sound astonished.

"C'mon! Like you don't know," Adya said sitting on the bed herself. *Distance shortens. Soon there will be none.* "She was all over you and you loved it!!'

Ashwin smiled and took a sip.

"God! Look at that grin!" Adya said irritated.

"What grin?"

"The same, I-am-such-a-charming-Indian-PM grin. The same, I-am-so-popular-with-girls grin."

Ashwin laughed.

"Don't laugh. You're known as the Indian Prime Minister popular among women."

"Look at the brighter side; such PMs are rare in India." He laughed.

"And what's rarer is a PM who equally likes the company of women," she added firmly.

"A womanizer, eh? " Ashwin stopped smiling.

"A womanizer is such a demeaning term for a Prime Minister, but then the Brussels incident and your intimacy with the Belgium Foreign Secretary is doing the rounds in the media."

"That was distorted! She had slipped and somebody clicked a picture and made a hullabaloo about it."

"Tell this to a woman down street. I am the editor in chief of a prestigious news group," she paused to take a sip of her drink.

"That photograph has *you* falling on her. Your face almost touching her face. I could dig that one out from my archive right now. How can you call it fake?" she added.

Ashwin looked at her.

"That lady was wearing one of those dresses which start from here," he said putting his hand over his chest. He was referring to a deep strapless dress. She was removing her jacket, and in the process she fell. I, being the closest, tried to help. It was then that somebody took that picture."

"If that's true, then why did you guys pay heavily to stop it from reaching the public," Adya said eyeing at him suspiciously.

"Lynnette is a respectable woman. I would not like her scandalous picture floating around."

Ashwin frowned, "See even if she was having an affair with me, how does it matter? Is it affecting our commitments towards our countries? No. Then why bother? Why make a fuss about it? That's our personal life. But we can't do that, can we? We have to create a fake aura around us to make people believe in us. It's human tendency to stereotype a profession or community. Can an Indian think of a Prime Minister in sweatshirts and loose pants, like I am wearing right now? In his mind, I even sleep in a khaadi kurta."

Adya laughed. Looking at him right now, nobody would believe he was head of a country!

"But you broke some stereotypes! You wore sunglasses to the rallies," she said looking amused.

"Initially I wore them for medical reasons. Later, I wore them because people loved them!"

"*Girls* loved it!" Adya corrected him.

"Ok! They make 50% of the Indian population. Got to keep them happy! Anything for the vote bank."

"You were the most eligible bachelor."

"What? Past tense?" Ashwin asked astonished. "I still am!"

"Narcissist, that's what you are."

"Whatever. If you had married me, you would have been the first lady of India and an object of envy."

"Could have. Did not. Not important now!" Adya sighed.

"I am really sorry for—" Ashwin began but Adya cut him short.

"Tell me how's Arun?" she quickly changed the topic. "Did he get married? Or you two?" she left the question hanging.

"He *did*!" Ashwin emphasized. "He married Prana."

"Oh? He used to date her!"

"Yes! And they have a beautiful girl named Bhavna who just won an international chess tournament in London."

"London, eh?"

"Yes!" Ashwin said enthusiastically.

"You sure keep a tab on Arun!"

"Both of us do! We keep in touch," Ashwin paused, and then as if he remembered something he asked Adya. "You looked happy when I said London. Why? "

"I live in London."

"Oh! Not in Alberta anymore?"

"Mom and Dad are still there," she finished her drink and got up. "I must leave now."

"What? Already?" Ashwin was visibly disappointed.

"We have to be at work tomorrow, Mr Prime Minister. Besides, I don't want anyone to raise an eyebrow."

"I understand," Ashwin pushed himself up wearily. "Are we going to meet tomorrow?"

"It depends. We both have tight schedules. Oh…which reminds me, can we have the interview?"

"Seriously?"

Adya nodded, "Will make it a quick one. We will have the questionnaire sent to your 'P-yar'. Pun intended!"

"I have to check my schedule." Ashwin laughed. "Only if time permits!" he added walking to the door with her.

Ashwin reached out to grab the door knob but did not open it. There was something in his head which was eating him up.

"Did you get married?" he asked directly. If she did not, they could meet again. If she did, he may be seeing her for the last time.

Adya studied him closely, and looked baffled. She then grabbed the door knob herself. "I simply couldn't." She opened the door and left.

Ashwin watched her leave as the security officer escorted her to the lift. She just couldn't marry! She must have tried. She must have been forced into relationships, but couldn't!

Will you wait?

I will

Ashwin never thought then that the wait would be for eternity.

Aaron Broody, senior correspondent for GNC, sent the final copy of Ashwin's interview for broadcast, and sat blankly.

Only a few months back, Aaron wanted to do a cover on Ashwin Jamwal. He was really excited to get a chance to interview him in Shanghai. Now he was repenting.

Aaron Broody was one of the finest journalists in GNC; his ability to hunt and eye for detail was unmatched. In his career of ten years, he had unearthed many secrets of people, places and businesses, many of which were covered and broadcasted. Besides his ability as a field journalist, he had Greek god looks and a very clear voice which made him a perfect fit for the primetime news anchor. GNC must have offered him that job many times; and many a times rival channels had offered him twice the pay to poach him; but he would always refuse. One does not refuse such offers, a TV anchor's position is a much safer job and the rival channel offered him financial security. But Aaron did, because in this office and in this position, he could always be close to *her* – the one, with whom he fell in love at first sight. The woman extraordinaire. Adya Batra.

Adya Batra was Aaron's superior in the organization. She must be over ten years older to him but, he didn't care for her age, ethnicity and position. All he saw was her eyes – beautiful, curious and expressive; and in moments of loneliness, pained.

In the last five years, he grabbed every opportunity to penetrate through the thick invisible wall which Adya had built around her, and tried to reach close to her heart. He thought he had been successful in breaking down the wall and they had something more than just professional congeniality.

Then Shanghai happened.

Aaron interviewed Ashwin Jamwal at the International Industry Conference. He read, through Ashwin's body language and expression, his feelings for Adya. It wasn't comforting. It was even more disturbing that Adya looked at peace. He thought the pain in her eyes was gone. Even though he always wanted to take away her pain, when it was gone, he didn't like it.

Aaron's body got warmer as his heart pumped more blood to match the adrenaline. *Fight or flight.* The strange feeling around his gut, on the one hand, was urging him to quit and leave because there was nothing left. *Flight.* And on the other hand, another feeling was prompting him to stay put. *Fight*

He rubbed his forehead with his palm, trying to ease the anxiety. He rested for a few minutes; his mind went blank as he finished his coffee. He needed some time to himself before he could take a decision. Finally he picked his phone.

"You asked me to do a story on Ashwin Jamwal sometime back, I am ready now! Though at a higher cost," he spoke on the phone.

"But what about your boss?" the voice spoke after some time. "The last time you bounced this idea, she rejected it!"

"Ignored," Aaron corrected. "And believe me, she won't ignore or reject it this time. There is a reason I am calling you after a long time."

"Well then I will make arrangements to transfer the amount… which would be?"

"I'll let you know in some time."

Taking money for an undercover report or sting operation to elevate or defame somebody is not new in media. Compared to other reporters in his league, Aaron had rarely indulged himself in such operations. Aaron never enjoyed paid operations but had done them, just for his survival. This time however, Aaron would put in all his energy and resources for the defamation of a different level.

"Ashwin Jamwal, your worst fears are about to come to life," Aaron said to himself.

♌

Ranjan Saxena rubbed his eyes and looked at the device in his hand once again. He had just spoken to Aaron Broody. Aaron had finally agreed to do a sting on Ashwin Jamwal. There could not be a better news.

Normally during the early hours of the evening, Saxena remained low, but not that day. That day he felt a spring coming back to his feet. He did not feel like a septuagenarian at all. He felt alive. Ashwin Jamwal had deprived him of something he loved most – power! With every passing day, Ranjan planned his revenge.

"Ashwin! You fool!" Saxena said out loud. "I am still living and I still have the power which I acquired myself. Unlike you…who was made powerful, was harnessed and jacked up to this position today. You are so engrossed in yourself that you can't fathom the power a person like me possesses, but very soon you will know! The curtains will be raised and you will learn the real meaning of power as your worst fears will come to life."

Ivan Kuruserv checked the equipment which would help him to locate Hades. He had been working on a project with Hades and Juan Carlos since the past five years

Juan Carlos died a week back.

Juan Carlos was spearheading major purchases from the European market. His services were not required in the last stages of project development, but Ivan felt his death was uncalled for. Ivan knew that Hades was behind the murder of the Kimetto brothers in the Andaman Sea. Now Juan was dead too. Ivan felt uneasy and wondered if he was destined to meet the same fate?

Ivan knew that Hades' obscurity was his biggest weapon and he was desperate to know about him. He was scheduled to have a video conference with Hades in five minutes. He had planned to use a highly advanced machine to track the correct IP location of the communicating device. Hades was heavily insulated; all his transmissions are diverted from a false IP address. Ivan had made many attempts to locate him in the past but had failed; he hoped to succeed that day.

If this highly sophisticated device used by Russian Intelligence couldn't locate Hades, nothing could, thought Ivan.

His system beeped and he accepted the VC request.

As usual, the screen was pitch dark. Not even a shadow!

"Even the real Hades did not wear the helmet of invisibility all the time, then why you?" Ivan laughed. "We have worked together long enough to trust each other—"

"Do you trust me?" Hades questioned sounding pleasant.

Ivan quickly glanced at the bottom of the screen to check the current IP location.

Tarapoto, Peru.

"I trust you enough to show you my face," he replied.

"But then I was the one to approach you, no?" Hades replied. "Besides, you can also choose the mask. Hardly matters to me. For me, our mission is important, not the faces of people involved."

"Then why the screen?" Ivan asked. He had to keep Hades engaged long enough for the device to give the correct location.

"Because it frightens. The fear of the unknown is the worst fear."

"So that's the only intention behind the obscurity?"

Kano, Nigeria.

"Nyet! It's the power to control," Hades spoke in Russian, Ivan's mother tongue. "Scared and threatened people are easily controlled."

"You speak Russian?" Ivan Kuruserv asked in English. "I didn't know that."

"One of my many talents!" Hades replied. "I thought you would be glad to talk in Russian, but you don't look pleased."

"I don't speak Russian anymore," Ivan replied flatly.

"Damaged permanently, eh?"

"Yes and *you know that!*" he said controlling his anger. "Deceived and betrayed by my own country"."

Ivan and his brother Boris were part of KGB. After the Cold War they both decided to quit the fast paced lives of intelligence officers and start afresh. It is unknown, if their actions were deliberate, but since the resignation coincided with the dissolution of the USSR and the subsequent split of the KGB, the Russian government feared they had defected to the CIA. After a few years, classified information started to leak and few KGB agents were compromised, affirming the Russian government's suspicion. Ivan and Boris had to be eliminated. Boris got a slow and very painful death, but Ivan survived with the memory of his brother dying in pain.

"Fifteen years of loyalty to a country, and they pay you by giving you a painful death," Ivan's hands were trembling. "Do you know Boris was in so much of pain that he actually started praying for death? The hospital authority strapped him so he could not commit suicide." Ivan sighed and wiped his eyes, trying to forget the painful memories. He then sat straight and continued. "There is no proof that we have defected but people with bloated egos sitting in plush offices at Moscow and Lubyanka couldn't accept a man leaving them for his own good. Those pigs sitting at the top flex their fingers and issue death orders. And this applies to Washington, London, Tokyo, Beijing – all the top men! They are all the same. Sadists. Defector or not, nobody, I repeat, nobody deserves to die like Boris."

"I understand. I am sorry I brought it up."

Raleigh, US.

"You asshole, you brought it up to instigate me! You bastard!"

"No such intentions, I am sorry," Hades said calmly.

"Shut up!"

Hades fell silent. He had done what he wanted to do. He had brought out all the hatred buried in Ivan's heart. Hatred, just like love, can make you do impossible things. Vengeance is the single motivation to perform the most difficult tasks in hand, under most untoward circumstances. Hades knew how to keep Ivan on track. He'd never let Ivan forget the painful death of his brother.

After a few minutes of silence, Ivan started updating Hades on the development of the project.

"More wait?" Hades exclaimed, once Ivan told him that the project may take more time to complete.

"It's not easy to make a deadly weapon of that scale. The research team is breaking its back since the last five years just to get the right product…"

"Five years! Man, we have grown old perusing our dreams."

"Not everyone. Juan Carlos is dead," Ivan said quietly. "And I feel you are responsible for it."

"I had ordered the killing of only the Kimetto brothers, that too only if they pull a stunt. Juan Carlos committed suicide."

"Why would Juan end his own life?"

Moscow, Russia.

"We live in an illusion more than in reality," Hades replied, "especially people like us. Guarded by fallacious thick iron walls, we feel protected. Then one day we are snapped into reality only to realize that the walls surrounding us are made of glass. Then we lose it, and start living in constant fear. With the slightest tremor, the fragile wall can break and will cut us deeply. With the control gone, men like us become vulnerable to even the drop of a pin. Juan saw the glass wall and he couldn't take it anymore. So he decided to end it all."

"I got it," Ivan spoke after a while. He imagined the scenario which Hades had just portrayed and began thinking, how long would his mind take to realize that the iron walls around him were made of glass?

He shook his head, "You should be a poet!"

"Aren't we all, in a way or the other." Hades laughed.

Moscow, Russia.

"Yes! We are in the process of writing a Divine Tragedy," Ivan laughed then asked grimly, "but you never told me why?"

"Why? What?"

"Why you want to do this? I want retribution, what's your reason?"

"I want power!"

"That you will have, once you will get hold of the weapon."

"Not that way!"

Moscow, Russia.

"What else?" Ivan said astonished. "With that weapon in hand, you can make those bastards on top chairs, run for their money. That's what I will do."

"Then you do it! My definition of control is slightly different."

"Is it?" Ivan frowned. "Are we on the same page?"

"Yes. Not the same purpose though. I want to be the most powerful man in the world. I don't want to control secretively. I want to disclose myself. What good is the power if nobody knows you have it?"

Moscow, Russia.

"You mean you will reveal yourself?" Ivan asked astonished. *Hades was a lunatic.*

"The most powerful person on earth."

"That's you…will be you."

"Yes!"

"So you are planning to actually go out in the open with a button for the weapon of mass destruction and shout 'Fear me, for I am the most powerful man'. Just like a comic book villain?" Ivan joked.

"Sounds interesting, but I still have some sanity left."

Moscow, Russia.

"So what's your plan?"

"I will defeat the most powerful person to become one. That's how I will disclose myself."

"Take my suggestion and go with the comic book version!"

"What's wrong with my plan?"

"Well to start with, the most powerful people are not the ones declared by the credit agencies; they are only constructions for the public. The real powerful people are the ones who work underground and are never seen on covers of magazines. That's what is wrong."

"That's why I will make one. And who knows, as we are talking, the most powerful person is getting made somewhere."

"We are talking humans here, right?"

"Yes! This operation will create the most powerful person in the world."

Moscow, Russia.

"And that won't be you?"

"Not until I defeat him or her."

"You're outrageous!"

"I am just trying to make my name."

"You will reveal yourself to the world soon, while you have not revealed yourself to us!"

"Who knows I did. You just failed to notice."

♌

Ivan disconnected the call and looked at the screen blankly. He noticed that the IP location had not changed for a long time. Moscow, Russia. Hades was based in Russia? How had he missed that! Ivan was anxious. He didn't trust his country anymore. If Hades was Russian, he may not want to work with him. It also dawned on him that it may be the reason why Hades was so secretive about his identity.

Just as he was about to disconnect, the button showing Hades' IP location blurred and changed to Delhi, India.

What the hell?

♌

Hades clicked and saw the blue ticker showing tracking of his IP. It blinked a little before changing to the original IP location. Delhi, India.

"Revelations, my friend, have already begun!" said Hades.

♞

Ashwin Jamwal was a little surprised to receive an invitation from the UN Counter Terrorist Convention in Geneva. India does not participate in such conventions. It only submits periodic reports on various security and counter terrorism methods to the Counter Terrorist Committee of the UN Security Council.

He settled on his designated seat and waited for the programme to begin. The heads of various states were still taking their places. A well-built man approached Ashwin and began checking all the machines kept at his seat. While pretending to work on the functionality of the console, the man passed him a card, stealthily.

Startled, Ashwin looked at the card. It had the UN Security Council logo at the top and was marked confidential. Ashwin immediately passed it to his National Security Advisor, Tahir Naqvi.

Tahir examined the card carefully before reading it; he wasn't happy with the anonymity of the message. The UN should have shared the message with him rather than the Prime Minister directly.

"What does it says?" Ashwin asked softly and Tahir read him the content.

Dear Mr Jamwal

You are requested to attend a meeting with the CTC special cell at 10:30 sharp. It's a highly confidential global security matter; hence we request your cooperation.

Sincerely,

Andrew D. Wakerfield
Director CTC

"That's it?"

Tahir nodded, checking the schedule of the programme – the Italian Prime Minister would take the stage at 10:30!

"I will get the authenticity of this thing checked," he said moving towards exit B.

Ashwin looked around the hall to see if someone else had got a similar invitation. The leaders were looking impatient, waiting for the programme to begin. Ashwin smiled briefly at some familiar faces and turned to check the schedule again. There was nothing unusual about it. The convention was supposed to start at 9:30 a.m. and end at 5:30 p.m. First, the director of CTC would speak about recent activities of the committee across the globe, which would be followed by speeches from various countries.

Tahir returned. "This is genuine," he said holding the card.

The programme began and the lights were dimmed. Barring a few coughs and the rustling of paper, there was no sound from the audience.

"So, I should go?" Ashwin whispered.

"They did not disclose the agenda of the meeting clearly to me," Tahir replied. "Something to do with global security. Looks like CTC will have a 1-0-1 with all the leaders."

"Oh God! I would like you to be ready with the latest reports on all our counter terrorist measures, cost statements, and expenditure breakup. Speak to the Defence Ministry and get the latest update," Ashwin said anxiously. "The UN should have these meetings with the defence heads, not us. Please get the reports fast; I want to check them before saying anything."

Tahir knew that Ashwin was a perfectionist and would not share an iota of information with anyone before validating it himself. Tahir started arranging for the reports while the conference went on, as scheduled. Finally the presenter called out for the Italian Prime Minister, and Tahir and Ashwin got up to leave.

Exit B led to a corridor. When they came out, there was nobody from the UN to assist them. For a few moments, they just stood there. Then the same man, who had given Ashwin the invitation, appeared from the left. He stopped a few steps before Ashwin, clearly surprised to see the cortege. Besides Tahir and Ashwin's Private Secretary Vidhan, six security personnel were also standing there…a total of nine people.

"Name is Mark Lawson, sir. I will be escorting you," he said smiling pleasantly. "This way," he said starting towards the right.

As they all started to follow him, he said, "Sir, you are with CTC. This is the most secure place on earth, at the moment."

Tahir got the drift and asked two security officers to stay back; he was not sure if Mark wanted him to get rid of everyone, but he couldn't take that risk. Mark did not comment and they continued to follow him through what seemed like a concrete maze. They were taking frequent turns.

"I spoke to the director, CTC about this meeting, and he said it is very urgent and pertaining to global security," Tahir said to Mark. "Nothing more."

"I am sorry sir, the agenda of the meeting is classified," Mark spoke as they took another turn and stopped at a dead end.

Tahir knew that wall must have a secret door or something; otherwise they all wouldn't stand there facing a freshly painted wall. And that's what it was. Mark placed his hand at a certain angle on a Jackson Pollock painting hanging on the wall; they all heard a lock click open as the wall went inside a little. Mark pushed it open.

Inside was a spacious room with a u-shaped conference table kept in the centre. The table could seat over twenty people, though most of the seats were vacant at that moment. Each seat had an inbuilt touch screen device which could interact with each other exclusively and could even share information by projecting it on the large screen mounted on the wall. It was hard to believe that such a sophisticated room could exist behind the walls of a normal building.

Ashwin smiled to nobody in particular and took the chair which Mark had graciously pulled for him.

The door opened a few more times, its clicks and hisses breaking the silence of that room. People were coming in and taking their places on the table; soon it was fully occupied.

Ashwin looked around the table, and he recognized five people immediately – they were the heads of France, Russia, United States, China and United Kingdom. Permanent members of the UNSC. He couldn't understand why he had been called for the meeting, though.

There were three other men who looked familiar. He must have seen them on the news or even met them, but he could not remember their names or designations. He didn't know most of the people sitting on that table. Then there were security personnel, standing behind respective leaders, and a few assistants from CTC. The room was full, but even then it had an eerie silence. Silence, was somehow comforting to everyone. Status quo has comfort.

Ashwin swivelled his chair slightly to the left, to face the latest occupant of that seat – the President of the United States, Anna Svenson. Anna noticed his movements and looked up. Ever since she had entered the room, she was busy on the interactive device. She looked confused and pensive, just like everyone else. She gave Ashwin her infamous smile and Ashwin smiled back.

Anna Svenson, the first female President of the United State, was as beautiful as elegant. She was tough, both mentally and physically and had proven that a woman can shine in any field. Her policies for the US and its inter-country relationships had been praised widely in the international media. She had been re-elected as president the second time and was named as one of the most iconic presidents in the history of USA.

Anna Svenson admired Ashwin Jamwal and had praised his policies and calibre on various international platforms. She felt good to see him sitting next to her.

The door opened one more time and a well-suited man in his mid-fifties walked in hurriedly. Ashwin didn't recognize him.

That man quickly took his position next to the screen. He called over one of the assistants and said something in his ear. The assistant nodded, and in a few minutes, CTC assistants ushered out the leaders' aides from the room before leaving themselves.

Tahir gave a slight nod to Ashwin as he passed him, signifying assurance. Security personnel were allowed to thoroughly check the room for safety before leaving. Tahir was satisfied.

After everybody left the room, the man cleared his throat. All the heads turned to face him. He was suited in black and wore rimless glasses which matched perfectly with his sophisticated attire. The man looked at the attendees and began,

"Respected gentlemen and honourable lady," he nodded at Anna, who nodded back in acknowledgement. "I sincerely apologize for the manner in which the meeting was arranged. I also understand the apprehensions regarding the security of the heads of states of six powerful nations."

Ashwin felt gratified to be included among six powerful leaders. Leaders of powerful nations! One and the same thing!

"But the matter is of such grave importance that we had to maintain high level secrecy and arrange for such a meeting in a jiffy. Hence, without further delay, let me introduce myself and purpose of the meeting." The man cleared his throat again. "My name is John Escrow and I am the director of a global counter terrorist organization called Global Anti-Terrorist Cell or GATC."

He paused again to let the information sink in. All the heads looked confused. Nobody had ever heard of such an organization. Escrow noticed the befuddled looks and continued.

"GATC was formed only seven years back when CTC realized that there is a steep rise in global terrorism. The world is at constant threat as the terrorists are becoming stronger. With increase in evil funding, terrorists across sects have enough access to the deadliest resources. From bio to nuclear, terrorists have broadened their expanse, putting the larger population at risk.

"CTC felt the need to take a more structured approach to counter terrorism. While the core team at CTC ensures that countries take apt counter-terrorist measures, another team was required to stop it at the global level. Hence GATC branched out of CTC. Owing to the risks involved in operation, the UN Security Council consciously decided to keep it a secret.

"A team of highly qualified professionals, including analysts and field agents operate in complete secrecy under the Defence Chief, post currently held by Mr Mervin Manuha." He said motioning his hand to his left, towards a black man. "Mr Manuha was earlier UNSC, Secretary for Counter Terrorism." Manuha smiled and nodded briefly.

Escrow continued, "The entire team reports to the Director, the post currently held by me." Escrow then sighed as if disappointed. "GATC planned to help in the culmination of terrorism across the globe, secretly, and we have been pretty successful till now."

"From where did you get funds?" Chinese President Yi Jifang interjected. He did not look happy. A secret organization was being operated, and the leaders were not aware of it! Jifang spoke for all.

"Well, CTC routed a certain amount of funding to GATC for operations," Escrow sighed, bowing his head slightly in guilt.

The leaders were angry and they showed no hesitation in exhibiting it. After a while, Manuha had to stand up and raise his hand. "I request you to please listen to us," he said over the non-comprehensible murmur. The room fell silent. Escrow took a seat closest to the screen and Manuha went up to the stage.

Mervin Manuha was a sixty-year-old short dark man with balding hair. He had an authoritative tone.

"We understand your concern about the routing of funds without your knowledge, but since global security was getting compromised, we refrained from leaking any information."

"And it is not compromised now?" Ashwin asked.

"Honestly, Mr Jamwal, given a choice, we wouldn't have shared it now," Manuha replied simply.

He was ready for this. The entire GATC team was ready for all the questions and accusations. "CTC may have manipulated balance sheets and secretly allocated funds, but sir, believe me, the funds have been utilized more efficiently and for a much bigger cause."

"I believe you," Jifang said bitterly.

"Further, *further*," Escrow emphasized, "fund utilization, since its inception, is maintained in the GATC, which is available for audit. We have nothing to hide," Escrow said a little firmly. "The intensity of global threat has reached another level and you will find about it in a while."

"Please speak!" spoke the Russian President Jahvn Fedyorov.

"The purpose of the meeting is to update you on a Weapon of Mass Destruction, which is being developed by a few individuals. These terrorists, as per our latest dope, do not belong to any organization. They are a few shrewd individuals, seeking retribution against the systems of the world."

"What kind of weapon?" asked Fedyorov.

"Nuclear!" Manuha replied.

"What the hell! A nuclear weapon requires lots of money and resources for development. It's not some dammed Heckler & Koch Automatic. It's a bloody W-M-D!" Anna said banging her fist on the table. "We take ages to develop a nuclear weapon and you are telling me a nondescript terrorist organization did that? Outrageous!"

"I wish I could deny it," Manuha said grimly, "But our intel is 100% correct. As per the dope, India and China will be heavily impacted with the fallout of WMD, owing to the large population spread all over the world."

Oh, so that's why I was called, thought Ashwin, because India is under the radar of nuclear attack. There goes the momentary feeling of pride and accomplishment in being included among the top leaders.

"You have got to be kidding us!" Chris Tanner, Prime Minister of UK cried. "I agree with Ms Svenson! Developing a nuclear weapon is next to impossible. You need experts, funding and…space! It's a bloody 1500 pounds weapon!" Chris exclaimed and then asked softly, "Can the radicals go to such an extent now?"

"Sadly, yes!" Manuha replied grimly.

"How did you find out about the weapon?" The quiet French President Alexei Lubont spoke for the first time.

"It all started when the Spanish ammunition mafia don, Juan Carlos, committed suicide a couple of months ago. Our field men in Europe had him under their lenses. The suicide seemed suspicious, so they began digging further and found out that only a few weeks before his death, his aides, including the famous Kimetto brothers, were killed in the Andaman Sea. Something wasn't right and our officers began following tracks to get more information on the deaths of the Kimetto brothers and their boss Juan Carlos. It turned out that Juan Carlos had indeed committed suicide, but the Kimetto brothers were killed while closing a deal on a nuclear warhead!" Manuha gulped. "We weren't sure of anything till our field men finally tracked down a man in Cuba. This man, named Ojas, was a transmitter working as a key between the financer in Fiji and Juan Carlos."

Manuha touched the screen on the wall. He then swiped the page twice, before stopping at the one which had a mug shot of a black man. Manuha started the slideshow and various images of that man, taken before and after the capture, started rolling on the screen. The 'before' pictures showed a healthy and well-dressed Ojas talking to various people in different locations. All were distant shots. The 'after' pictures had Ojas in a blue prison uniform. There were some pictures where he was being interrogated by a few officers in a dark room. Though the pictures depicted only normal interrogation approaches, there was no denying of the fact that extreme measures had been adopted for interrogation, because Ojas had lost lots of weight and his body was bruised.

All the leaders noticed that but remained quiet so Manuha continued.

"Ojas spilled the beans after hours of interrogation," Manuha said. "He revealed that some of the raw materials for the weapon were brought into Juan Carlo's hub in Cuba. From there, the half processed materials were sent to various locations. Where? He doesn't know. And we believe him. This is how Juan Carlos always operated, making people like Ojas work exclusively for one activity. This minimizes the risk and does not impact the procurement and disbursement chain.

"Ojas used to update the key financer in Fiji, who in turn would take it forward. Ojas and his people have also transported some of the raw material to Fiji—"

"Everything could be so wrong!" Anna interjected. "These men… these transmitters exaggerate everything!"

"I agree." Ashwin nodded. "These people work only on obligations. They need to believe they are part of a bigger agenda. Just because some illicit trading of suspicious raw material happened, it doesn't mean that a nuclear warhead is being developed!"

"I think it is unprofessional on your part to involve all of us based on such a trivial lead by a transmitter," Anna said angrily.

"No Madam, we would never do so," Manuha replied grimly. "We have the same integrity as the United Nations. Had the situation been a bit under our control, we would have not called all of you," he paused for a second and then added, "Ojas gave us the name of the mastermind."

"Who?"

"A man name Ivan Kuruserv."

"A Russian?" Fedyorov, the Russian President sat up.

"A terrorist, sir! They do not belong to a country or religion," Escrow replied. "We did a background check on Ivan; he was a former KGB operative. His brother and he were accused of defecting to CIA in 1992. While his brother died under mysterious circumstances, he disappeared from the face of the earth. Ojas' description of Kuruserv and his modus operandi matches with the data we have. We have studied Ivan closely and we believe that not only does he have access to resources and information, but he also has knowledge about carrying out a nuclear attack."

He had the undivided attention of everyone and whatever little doubt the leaders had seemed to be vanishing now. "We have other middlemen and transmitters affirming the possibility of nuclear warhead development and Ivan's connection with the same," he added.

The room was quiet.

"We have been trying to locate the weapon as well as the mastermind, but with the murder of Muniz, the Fiji entrepreneur who was acting as financer and a middleman between Juan Carlos and Kuruserv, we reached our cul-de-sac. He was our only link to Ivan," Manuha said with dejection in his voice. According to the intel, the attack will happen on the 24th of June."

In less than two months.

"Did Ojas tell you about the agenda?" Alexie Lubont, the French Prime Minister, asked. "Who is the target?"

"Looking at the estimated amount of raw material that has been traded, it seems more than one nuclear weapon is getting developed," Manuha replied

'Impact?'

"Over 35% of global population, directly or indirectly."

"Close to four billion?" Alexei gulped.

"Not to forget the deformities in F2 generations!"

The room fell silent and then there was chaos as all the leaders started talking at the same time. Different accents, different phrases but similar questions. What next?

Escrow took the stage again. "Even one such attack will be a huge blow. People will start living on the edge. While it will promote new age radicalism, old extremist groups will also rise to power. Governments and organizations such as UN will lose control forever. Economies will fall and a war of a different league could start."

Everyone looked tensed. John Escrow pursed his lips and began, "This is a time of crisis and the entire world population is at risk. We cannot afford to have a fragmented approach to the whole situation. GATC will require access to the information from each country and permission for our field men to operate in your country. I request you to work together and think of the world as one; just for this one mission."

Escrow noticed that the leaders did not look pleased. This would take some time. Three thousand years of territorization could not be forgotten like that! But the world had never faced a crisis like this before and Escrow could only pray.

The meeting was adjourned after introducing other members from the GATC. It included the head analyst, director of operations, and nuclear scientist among others. These people would directly approach leaders, if the situation demanded.

While everybody walked towards the door, something crossed Ashwin's mind and he approached Escrow.

Before he could speak, Anna Svenson pitched in.

"Mr Escrow, I apologize for being harsh," she said coming forward.

"It's fine, Ms Svenson. I understand the pressures. I would have reacted the same way." Escrow replied looking at both Anna and Ashwin.

"It is not comforting to know that radicalism has reached this stage. What an irony! While we nations keep increasing our defence budget to protect our boundaries from each other, we are threatened by people living in our own country. A terrorist just has to press a button and our border forces will be of no use. Still we spend on building up our armed forces." She sighed. "It reminds me of Eisenhower famous speech: Every gun that is made, every warship launched, every rocket fired signifies, in the final sense, a theft from those who are hungry and are not fed, those who are cold and are not clothed." She smiled wearily.

She suddenly realized that Ashwin had been standing there all the while. "I am sorry Mr Jamwal. You were here to speak to Mr Escrow and I just barged in." She said apologetically

"No problem," Ashwin smiled. "I was here with same thought as yours."

Anna smiled.

Ashwin added, "Just one more thing which crossed my mind," he asked Escrow. "I was thinking how a man so well-insulated all these years, will let the plan surface just before the attack? Maybe Ojas was planted so you could find him! Is it possible?"

"Unfortunately, it seems possible now," Escrow said anxiously. "Why did we not think of that?"

"What?" Anna asked.

"That we are being controlled," Ashwin replied.

"And I don't want to think about anything else now!" Escrow said as he opened the door for both the leaders.

For the next a few weeks, Ashwin frequently travelled abroad for GATC meetings, under the cover of international conferences or bilateral discussions. To avoid global scale panic, all heads had consciously decided to keep the news of the possible terrorist attack limited to a close circle. Except for NSA, Tahir Naqvi and the Defence Minister Prabhakar S., nobody knew about the crisis. Ashwin's frequent travels were noticed and were vehemently condemned by both the media and opposition. He was helpless and couldn't do anything about it. On top of that, the top intelligence agencies in the world had failed to track Ivan Kuruserv. What was even more exasperating was that they could not locate a weapon weighing over a thousand tonnes!

While his country was against him, even the GATC meetings were not as productive as they should have been. This global emergency could only put all of them in one room, but even in such a crisis, frequent moments of tension of ongoing relationships among the nations could be felt. Their meeting that day came to standstill, when Anna and Jahvn started comparing the competence of their respective intelligent agencies. The discussion heated up and Manuha had to step in and pre-close the meeting. If only all the nations could work as one unit, thought Ashwin. But it is not going to happen, he knew that.

Ashwin looked at his watch, it was 3:30 p.m. and Adya would be coming anytime. He was in Scotland. His flight back home was due the next day. Adya was travelling from London to meet him. He wished he could share the crisis with her.

Ashwin was pulled out of his thoughts as Adya was ushered in.

"Finally, we have met because *I* travelled, *again!*" she said bitterly after the security left the room. She had travelled the second time in a row to meet him. Ashwin had ditched her at the last moment before their meeting in Peru.

"And a hello to you too..." Ashwin smiled.

"I am not pleased!" Adya said throwing her handbag on an armchair.

Ashwin replied, "I hope I can help."

"You have been quite a help already," she said sitting on a chair across Ashwin

"You know there is buzz in the media about Indian PM and his secret 'someone'?" Adya pulled out her phone from her bag and then began reading from the device.

"Ashwin Jamwal is overlooking national affairs because he is starting a new one for himself. When the country is going through serious trouble, he is frequently travelling abroad just to meet his secret someone under the cover of international trade conferences."

She continued with fake voice modulation, "And we wonder, who is this secret someone for whom the Indian Prime Minister is ignoring his own country?"

Ashwin laughed.

"Seriously!" Adya said firmly, "What's going on? Because we are not meeting and yet there are rumours."

"What made you think *you* are the secret someone?" Ashwin said, his eyes studying Adya. She could be a high profile media person, but inside, she was still that easily excitable girl from Allahabad. "I am seeing someone else!" Ashwin added seriously.

It was Adya's turn to laugh and she laughed from the heart. She finally stopped laughing and wiped her tears before speaking again, "Seriously. What's going on?" Ashwin only smiled so she continued grimly, "You know, the opposition has got enough dirt on you, only because of this month. There is some crisis in the East and I have heard that you have cancelled the meeting at the very last moment and left the matter hanging! You are travelling extensively to random conferences, many of which you do not attend. Even your cabinet is not pleased with you. There is visible hatred against you in your ministry and I don't blame them. They are clueless about the activities of their leader. You will not be elected next time at this rate."

"I don't want to be elected next time!"

Adya raised her brows and continued, "If things continue like this, you may even have to step down! The East crisis is growing bigger every day, and you cannot just shrug it off," Adya said studying Ashwin. He looked tired and unwell. There was a faint smell of balm in the room; he must have had headache.

She remembered he suffered from migraine headaches, since childhood. Earlier during such attacks, he used to close himself in his room and sleep for hours. Now he had to work. She felt sorry for him. "I wish I could do something about this!"

Ashwin said drinking some water. "It has been projected that I have aggravated the crisis, by not being physically present. You are a member of the press; you would know a situation or crisis is evaluated by experts in the PM office. Deliberations on the crisis are made without the PM. My physical presence is immaterial. I was appraised about the situation while I was travelling; I gave my feedback, but the cabinet did not act on it," Ashwin said exasperated.

"You have become far too big for their liking. Your own cabinet is using it as an excuse to pull you down. Take control of the situation!"

Ashwin was about to reply when the phone kept near the study table rang. He got up unsteadily. He was tired.

"The President of the United States would like to have a conversation," said the voice on phone.

"Please patch," Ashwin said. The line went dead and there were a few beeps before he heard Anna Svenson's voice.

"Mr Jamwal? I hope I am not interrupting anything important."

"Nothing much," Ashwin said looking at Adya. He disengaged the phone and took it to the next room.

"I have called to apologize for what happened in the meeting today," Anna said.

"With Jahvn?"

"Yes, we wasted a lot of time." She paused briefly, expecting Ashwin to add something. He didn't, and she got the drift. Ashwin was not happy with the way the meeting had ended. "I am not justifying, but it's not easy to give up your instincts! The moment your enemy attacks, you counter attack, not defend, but retaliate. That's what happened today when Fedyorov spoke against the CIA."

"I understand," Ashwin replied slowly, "But in an attempt to fight for power, aren't we ignoring the fact that if that man presses the button, Russia or the US would cease to exist? Shouldn't we be acting right now and not debating? We are making it difficult for Escrow."

"I know!" Anna emphasized. "I also know it's difficult to get the CIA and FSB to work together."

"We don't have a choice!" Ashwin replied. "Besides, our field men are wiser than us, and are not driven by egos. They believe in operating for a cause while the leaders believe in control. We operate for our impactful existence rather than cohesive survival. The only reason FSB, CIA and RAW could never work together is because we don't want them to." He paused briefly to remind himself that he was speaking to the US president Anna Svenson and then continued softly. "Time is passing swiftly and we have to act fast. Trust me, I know it's difficult, but at times we have to keep our egos at bay."

"Like I always say that you are very honest. If you want an unbiased opinion, Ashwin Jamwal is the man," Anna said after some time.

"Well thanks, I am not proud of this virtue, though," Ashwin replied smiling.

"Yes! The clock is ticking and we haven't found any concrete lead, yet."

"We are dealing with a shrewd individual."

"I remember you said that a terrorist is controlling events around us," Anna Svenson said, "but that is only possible if an insider is helping him."

"Infiltration? It is possible, but the risks are high. Remember there are six intelligence agencies working on the case. A small mistake would put the whole nation in jeopardy."

"And the GATC members have impeccable track records with UNSC, but then how is he controlling us?"

"By giving us only that bit of information which he wants us to know." Ashwin sighed. "That mastermind, Ivan, had been an intelligent agent himself and could work surreptitiously under our noses; it's not something he is doing for the first time."

"Other radical organizations could be assisting him."

"Yes, he is not doing it alone."

"That's not good news. I wish it'd all fall in the right place," Anna said.

"I wish that too," Ashwin said. "I also wish that the next time the President of the US calls, it is for the merging of economies, and not about some maniac with a WMD!"

Anna laughed. She needed a break from the tension and was grateful to Ashwin for that.

"Or the next call could be for a dinner date!" she said smiling.

"A dinner date followed by the drafting of some policies on merging our economies!" Ashwin laughed and disconnected the call.

He spent another half an hour calling people in his office, and then he called Tahir for an update.

♌

Ashwin was on the phone for almost two hours. When he was done, he found Adya lying on his bed, watching an Indian news channel.

"Don't you get tired of this?" Ashwin asked falling wearily on the couch.

"I make my living out of it!" Adya said turning the TV off. "Don't you get tired of what you are doing?"

Ashwin did not reply as something crossed his mind. Anna Svenson seemed correct about the infringement. There could be a traitor in the group; and if that was the case, the intelligence services were just wasting time. He was so lost in his thoughts that he did not notice Adya sitting next to him, till she touched his right arm.

"Here, have this," she said passing a glass of scotch to him. "Everything okay?"

"Everything is fine," Ashwin said slightly dazed. "I was just thinking about the East crisis," he said taking a sip. He desperately needed that drink

"You don't look well," Adya touched his forehead. "You had a migraine attack today?"

Ashwin nodded, astonished. How did she know?

"I am fine…just tired."

"There is something troubling you. Tell me, maybe I can help," Adya said, gently rubbing his back.

"I am tired, that's it."

"You do not go into a conversation with the President of the US on a sterile line, if everything's fine. Don't tell me you were having an intimate conversation with her?" Concern was written all over her face.

"As a matter of fact, Anna Svenson asked for a dinner date."

"Oh? She called you on a sterile line for a dinner date?" Adya said sarcastically

"I think she *likes* me!"

Ashwin noticed the apprehension on Adya's face and decided to push his luck further, so he whispered, "She is the secret someone!"

Adya stiffened at once, so Ashwin said, "You are still that girl from Allahabad. Not grown up a bit!" he said holding her hand.

"And you are still that same boy! Not changed, at the age of ten you behaved like sixty! You still do," Adya said smiling, remembering

Ashwin when he was young. "When memories come, they are so vivid. Remember we used to sneak out of our houses in the lazy summer afternoons to play cricket in that shabby park? There were so many buffaloes, but we would still play."

"I remember!" Ashwin said smiling, "If a ball hits a cow, you are out!"

He laughed. "I so wish we could go back to those times. But everything is changed now." Ashwin sighed and picked up his drink.

"If it is of any consolation, Aaron will be in Allahabad. He is doing a cover on you. I have asked him to revisit all our special places."

"Aaron? Who?"

"Aaron Broody assists me. The same dude who interviewed you in Shanghai!"

Of course Ashwin knew who Aaron Broody was. In that interview he saw admiration for Adya in Aaron's eyes. He just wanted to know Adya's feelings about him. Nothing.

♌

Manuha also received a call from Anna Svenson regarding her argument with Jahvn; she was apologetic and he understood.

"We don't have time; we should, act fast," Manuha replied and disconnected the phone.

He then took a piece of paper and made a check list:

Tracing Juan Carlos's death	(√)
Convincing CTC core team	(√)
Ojas arrest and revelation (√)	
Finalizing date of destruction	(√)
Making a power packed team	(√)

Manuha looked at the sheet, tore in into small pieces and then ate it.

Aaron Broody reached Allahabad an hour late as his flight from Delhi was delayed due to a technical glitch in the aircraft. Adya had asked an acquaintance to help him in Allahabad.

Aaron did not need assistance in Allahabad, or in any other city. Even though his Delhi assistant was a resourceful man, with access to all the politicians of the country, he wasn't exactly a help. He was Ashwin's loyalist and showed only his positive side. Aaron had to work double hard to dig out some dirt on Ashwin.

Aaron found his assistant, Harshit Varma, the instant he came out of the airport. It wasn't difficult to spot him, mainly because there were very a few people standing at the exit with a name placard. His assistant wasn't even holding one. He was holding a pink sheet with his name scribbled in blue ink.

Pink? For who else but me.

Adya knew Harshit's father. He was her senior in the university. She told Aaron that Harshit was the right man for the job. He knew the city like the back of his hand. What she didn't tell him was that Harshit was very young and very talkative.

While driving back from the airport, Harshit talked incessantly. He told him that his car is the best. He commented on the poor condition of the roads. He would point at some random shop and would describe its legacy. He talked about parks and rivers. He told Aaron about the dating scene in Allahabad. He talked about his girlfriend and his family. He talked about the English Mastiff next door.

Everything!

But Aaron wasn't listening. He was thinking about the progress of his report. It wasn't good. Aaron had been in India for a fortnight. He had checked the archives, spoken to the Opposition, did a sting on Nationalistic Party members, but couldn't gather enough meat. He decided he would consolidate all the information and see where he stood that day. He may have to adopt a different approach; he may have to start afresh. He felt depressed. Only four months back he was planning to propose Adya and give her all the happiness in the world. Now he is in Allahabad, just because he saw her happy, but not *with him*. Not because of him. That's where it all started. The human mind becomes most destructive when it loves, because then it stops rationalizing, and also when it hates, because then it stops functioning.

Aaron loved Adya and hated Ashwin to the core.

"When will we reach?" asked Aaron, finally.

"We are almost there," Harshit said taking a turn. "I took a longer route."

"What?" Aaron said loud enough to scare the boy. "Why?" and shook his head.

Harshit did not reply, he slowed the car after a few minutes "I took a longer turn, because I wanted to show you Adya didi's house," he said, happily pointing at an old two storey house on Aaron's left.

The house looked inhabited, but poorly maintained. The paint of the wall was peeling out. The garden did not have flowers, but it was neat. Aaron imagined little Adya running in the garden, yelling out of the big terrace and felt ecstatic.

Harshit leaned over to look at the building himself, "I knew you would like it."

"Yes. Thank you so much," Aaron said, still looking at the building. "And I am sorry."

"No problem, sir," Harshit said taking his position. "Now if you look to your right." Aaron turned and saw another house a few feet away.

"That is Ashwin bhaiya's house," Harshit added. "That's why the security!"

"Let's go now. I am tired"

♌

After settling in the hotel, Aaron decided to sort the important stuff from the material he had gathered. After hours of scrutinising and sorting, Aaron looked at his final folder and felt devastated. There were a very a few files. He went through them again:

Blackmailing was his secret weapon, actually it still is! – Day 3. Udaipur, state leader, Opposition party.

The dissolution of two major PSUs was done to promote a private organization, which heavily funded the Nationalistic party. Those PSUs could have been saved, but the decision came in less than two weeks. Major layoff, people lost jobs and Central government filled their pockets. – Day 5. Delhi, Former Principal Secretary to PM.

And...

At times he would just disappear. He would pull down an iron sheet and there is no way to connect to him. Then he'd be back as if nothing happened. That's his way of de-stressing, but it becomes enduring for people like us, waiting for his decision. – Day 7. Delhi, Clerk PMO.

And some more.

He is running away from East Crisis to save his ass. He doesn't know whom to support. Either way, he is going to lose the vote bank, so he's trying to play it safe. We fear worse. There are evidences that connect Ashwin to the largest terrorist organization in the east. – Day 12. Delhi. Member, opposition party.

He has underworld connection. I don't have proof. You find it. – Day 10. Delhi, opposition party member.

Aaron could swear it was his worst work till date. He knew he didn't have a lot of content, but he had no idea that the quantity was so little! Almost zero! Does this man have no negative side? A thought crossed Aaron's mind, starting an uncomfortable dull pain from his oesophagus to the stomach. Ashwin had brought India to the global map, in terms of economic policies and education. There may be some reforms or policies which could have benefitted him or some other party he is obliged to; but in the broader context, all those reforms have profited the country more. Nobody gets a second term majority like he did. There must be something about this man.

The recording of a female supporter played in his mind out of nowhere. The woman went on praising Ashwin Jamwal for a good five minutes, starting from his model-like looks and his attire, to his infamous sunglasses, his smile, his attempt to break stereotypes and his good sense of humour. She excessively used superlatives to describe each attribute.

Aaron made a mental note to delete that file.

♌

The next day, Aaron met Ashwin's mother. Adya had arranged the interview. It was pointless! The kind of information that he was looking for would never come from proud parents. He only went there to get names of a few relatives. Ranjan Saxena had tipped him – 'if you want dirt, speak to jealous relatives'. Aaron was disappointed; his project had come down to family politics.

Aaron recalled the conversation he had had with Mrs Jamwal. He found her warm and very intellectual. He could have conversed with her all day, had she not been Ashwin's mother. Smiling throughout, she fondly remembered her son's childhood.

There were moments of hesitation and Mrs Jamwal looked uncomfortable when Aaron asked her about the sacrifices Ashwin had to make to become an icon.

"I think…Adya," she replied but Aaron sensed the doubt in her voice.

Adya was not sacrificed; she wasn't in the agenda.

For the next one week, Aaron worked nonstop. Torn between duty and revenge, many a times he felt he lost track on both counts. He visited places where Ashwin had left his footprints – starting from his school and the university campus to the intersections and parks. He visited all; gathered nothing.

♌

Aaron would call his meeting with Ashwin's 'distant relative' a productive one. It led to something, if nothing else; it was good enough to shatter Ashwin. Aaron smiled to himself as he went through all of Ashwin's family pictures that he had taken from Ashwin's mother.

The news is verified.

Such big news had been hidden for more than forty years; Aaron made a mental estimate of the price this information could fetch him. He would not share it with Ranjan Saxena. This piece of info could make him a millionaire overnight. He just needed the right buyer.

He called Harshit and his friend Ankur for drinks. He was going to celebrate.

They were at the hotel bar.

After a few rounds of drinks, Harshit asked Aaron, "You like Adya didi?"

"She is my boss. I admire her," Aaron replied avoiding eye contact.

"Not that way. *Love* her?"

Aaron did not reply.

"I can see that in your eyes. Your face lights up every time we talk about her," Harshit said motioning the waiter for more drinks. "I also smile every time Vishakha's name pops up in any conversation. Even if I see a 'masala' brand named Vishakha I feel butterflies in my stomach. That's love." Vishakha was the name of Harshit's girlfriend.

"No. That's gas," Ankur said immediately. Aaron laughed, relieved at the interruption.

Harshit scowled at them and asked Aaron again, "How do you find Vishakha?"

Aaron had met Vishakha numerous times.

"Oh. She is beautiful, intelligent and caring, and I can say she knows what she wants from life. Seriously, I feel she could have done better than you."

"Sir!"

"Joking! She loves you a lot because she never complained that you are not giving her enough time because of me."

"I see you as an elder brother I always wanted. Why would she complain, if I am spending time with my brother?"

Brother? Aaron looked at Harshit; he wasn't joking and meant each word he said.

The next day when Aaron started his interview with Arun's mother, he had a bad hangover. Arun's mother Kakoli Roy Deb was a chattier version of Ashwin's mother. After a casual chit chat, Aaron began, "Since how long have you known Ashwin Jamwal?"

This question was posed to validate the information, which could fetch him millions.

"Since forever," she replied smiling. "You know, Ashwin's mom and myself, we have been friends for fifty years," she added without being asked.

"So your friendship trickled down to the boys?"

"God knows! We didn't see that coming. The boys have been friends for nearly thirty-five years."

Aaron made a note.

"I have never seen a friendship like theirs," she smiled again.

"Just like their mothers."

"Not exactly. Friendship between women are practical because we rationalize, prioritize. For, us our family's interests and inclinations come first. But for boys, there is nothing like that. They think from the heart and act. Arun and Ashwin had this *bromance*. They still have. Do you know they are still regularly in touch, even though both are very busy people, especially Ashu? Last year Arun met with a minor accident. Ashu called him from New Delhi and they both talked all night! We felt that from that day, Arun recovered twice as fast."

"Mr Jamwal likes your son a lot?" Aaron asked.

"Oh, Arun also likes Ashwin. Arun has always been loyal to Ashwin. He is like his protector and Ashwin has always known that."

"Known what?" Aaron interrupted.

"That Arun is behind his success, starting from his school days. While Ashwin focussed on agenda, Arun worked inconspicuously and eliminated any hurdle, any risk, which might arise in the course of action."

"Is it?" Aaron said surprised.

"Yes. Ashwin's ambitions were Arun's ambitions."

"But he remained a sidekick." Why did Aaron use that word! He couldn't take it back!

"The word is stalwart," she replied firmly. "If you start moving closely with them, you will know Arun is the stronger and powerful one."

Arun's mother gave Aaron enough dump to keep him busy for the next three days. He met people, visited places and at the end found that Arun indeed, was a strong force behind Ashwin.

Aaron joined Harshit for a smoke under a huge neem tree, opposite the science faculty. They were waiting for Vishakha. Aaron planned to leave Allahabad in two days' time; he had got what he was looking for.

"I am sorry, you have to wait!" Harshit said sipping his tea.

"I'm enjoying myself. It's very refreshing to stand here and observe people," Aaron said looking at a bunch of students. "Besides, Vishakha has waited for us every time. We can do this at least once."

"There she is!" Harshit beamed as he saw Vishakha coming out of the science faculty gate with her friends. Aaron waved at her and she began crossing the road.

She increased her pace and was slightly ahead of her friends when a motorbike drove past her at a ridiculously high speed. One of the girls shrieked and Aaron saw Vishakha falling. It all happened in a matter of seconds. They both rushed to Vishakha, who was writhing in pain on the street. What Aaron saw that day, will haunt him for life.

Vishakha's face was shrivelling revealing her muscles and veins. Somebody had thrown acid on her.

They rushed her to the hospital and Aaron stayed with Harshit. Harshit was in complete shock. He did not speak, cry, eat or drink. He just sat outside the ICU and waited until the doctor told them that she was out of danger.

"Can we see her now?" Harshit spoke for the first time. The doctor nodded slowly.

Harshit went inside and came back immediately. He covered his face with his hands and burst into tears.

"She is going to be okay," Aaron said, making him sit on a chair. He then gave him water which Ankur had brought.

"Who could do such a thing?" Aaron asked finally.

"A boy named Rohit," Ankur replied. "Rohit has told everyone in the hostel that he loves Vishakha. Rohit spilled acid on her just because she likes Harshit instead. Poor Vishakha, she doesn't even know that Rohit has feelings for her!"

Aaron felt a pain in his chest. The story was so similar to his.

"It's my fault," Harshit said before sobbing again.

♌

Aaron was packing to leave, when Ankur called and told him that Vishakha had tried to commit suicide. She did not want to live with a distorted face.

He rushed to the hospital. Harshit was standing against the wall opposite the ICU. Vishakha's mother was crying continuously.

Aaron stood next to Harshit while Ankur knelt beside Vishakha's mother. Nobody spoke for the next half an hour. Finally the doctor came out. She looked at the group, shook her head and walked away. A stretcher followed, carrying Vishakha's body covered with a white sheet. Harshit saw the stretcher and fainted.

♌

Aaron first emailed his resignation and then called Ranjan.

Ranjan was baffled with the news.

"I thought you'd find something that would bring Ashwin down to his knees," said Ranjan irritated.

Aaron had already found that.

'I thought you will find who is behind Ashwin's success?' Ranjan Added

He had found that too.

"It doesn't matter anymore. Any of this," replied Aaron before hanging up.

Tahir Naqvi came out from the conference room looking flustered.

"Someone is busy connecting with Langley and Lubyanka every day," Naqvi heard Ashwin's voice the moment he entered the adjoining room.

"Au contraire, I was with Beijing!" Naqvi replied in irritation. He had been on the phone for four hours!

"Why the sad face? I thought you always wanted to work with other international intelligence agencies and compare them to RAW!"

"I am not proud of it; almost embarrassed!" Tahir replied sadly. "The truth is, even with this entire hullabaloo about our defence expenditure, RAW is nowhere close to the CIA or FSB."

"You once claimed that RAW is equivalent to KGB."

"No. But we could be, if the government allocates more funds to intelligence services."

Ashwin laughed, adding to the frustration of the National Security Advisor

"Ever since I have been appointed NSA, I am persuading the government to pour more funds into RAW, but the government is paying no heed to my request."

"Perhaps the government does *not* have funds!" Ashwin said.

"Or because they're all going into Swiss accounts," Tahir replied. "It has always been like that! Defence will manage, military will manage. Surprisingly, we do manage; and just because we manage doesn't mean we get enough support. I am disheartened at the approach. I mean, it's okay if the government doesn't have funds; have empathy, at least!" Tahir said pacing up and down the room.

"But even that is too much to ask," he continued. "And then the government is looking for excuses to minimize the funding: RAW officers are paid too well, RAW is autonomous, RAW does not believe in reporting structure. Yes, we prefer to work discreetly! National security is our priority; you cannot expect us to report everything. Besides we don't trust these bureaucrats, they can even sell our country for self-interest. While we are under constant heat, the ministers sit in AC offices and fill their pockets. If a mission is successful, everyone takes the credit, but if it fails, the NSA is blamed. He faces the fire. Then we—" Naqvi paused as he noticed Ashwin staring at him. Tahir moved over to the table, picked the glass of water and drank it. Even though he was speaking the truth, at the end of the day, he was reporting to Ashwin.

"You can check my Swiss account," Ashwin spoke after a long glare, 'If you could find one."

"That doesn't imply to you. None of it," Naqvi said. "You are the best we have!"

"But then I am not," Ashwin sighed, "Howsoever I try, I will always be a part of that corrupt-Indian-politician pool!"

"No. No," Naqvi said empathetically. "I could truly say that you are the best PM ever, if I didn't know that you initially wanted Arun Deb to be the NSA." He smiled.

"Says the NSA of India," Ashwin replied smiling. "For how long do I have to live with this? I only recommended Arun, because besides being my best friend, he has an impeccable record."

"He is ten years less experienced than me!"

"And that's why you are here," Ashwin said pressing a button on his phone. "Please call Vidhan and send some tea for Mr Naqvi and myself," he spoke on the phone.

"I desperately need some tea!" Tahir said.

"So? What's the news from Beijing?" Ashwin asked massaging his temple with his fingers.

"Not good!" Tahir replied sadly. "We are using our best strategies and our best men, but we still haven't got anything!"

"What?" Ashwin sat up. "Is this the best the world's top most intelligence agencies can do? Nothing! How hard can this be?' he asked angrily.

"That's the problem. We are expected to deliver exceptional results in no time! I am sure right now my fellows from MI, CIA and FSB are also getting similar responses from their bosses. Our bosses expect us to deliver results the moment they issue orders."

"Our point is how long will it take for top intelligence agencies to locate a thirty foot weapon?"

Naqvi spoke sadly, "I don't know"

"So buckle up!"

"We are so tight that we may choke!" Tahir replied defensively. "We have tried everything under the sun. We now feel the weapon doesn't exist!"

"Doesn't exist?" Ashwin frowned "Or have your drones failed to penetrate?"

Tahir looked at him, pained at the remark.

"All the agencies have come to the same conclusion."

"Are you even listening to yourself? Is that even possible with all the proofs and the evidences?

"The intel was given by the GATC team and we are beginning to think that they only have planted it."

"I am getting wary of this discussion," Ashwin replied confused. "Why would any conscientious organization linked to the United Nations adopt such means? What's their gain?"

"Perhaps they were looking for an excuse to come out into the open."

"By risking the rectitude of the entire United Nations?" Ashwin said looking at his watch. He had a meeting to attend, shortly, and Vidhan would be bringing the agenda. "I still think you all are overlooking the finer details."

"I don't know!" Tahir said anxiously, "but then the question arises – why any individual or group would do it? Our FOs are chasing some leads, so let's see."

"Fast!" Ashwin said, "Whatever, we need to close it soon. We have other issues to attend to."

Tahir was about to reply when Vidhan entered with a few documents in his hand. He noticed the flushed look on Tahir's face and immediately knew that Ashwin was not in a good mood.

"Sir, the Finance Minister has asked for your signature on all these documents. He also asked you to join them for a meeting on the East crisis tomorrow."

"Tell Dhananjay to put his head where it belongs!" Ashwin replied angrily. "And for God's sake, am I supposed to dance on the East crisis now? I have given the verdict and signed the policy agreement. What now?"

Vidhan did not reply. He was not supposed to. Instead, he started briefing Ashwin about each document he had to sign.

"See, I am not sitting idle here," Ashwin said in frustration, after signing the last document. "I will be flying to London after two days. I have some international issues to look at! Then I have existing issues that need my attention. I can only work as much as my body permits. I am not a machine. My body is giving up now!"

"I am sorry, sir. I know something crucial is going on, but sadly the cabinet doesn't think so," he said softly.

"Something crucial is indeed going on, son. But it is something that we will manage. Tell the ministers in the cabinet to trust him," Tahir replied instead. He knew that Ashwin would reprimand Vidhan for his audacious remark, but Vidhan only said so, because he liked

Ashwin a lot. It must be getting harder for him to face the heat from the begrudging cabinet ministers, everyday. He just wanted to apprise Ashwin of the situation.

"To hell with the cabinet," Ashwin said angrily and then vented out his frustration against the cabinet's approach for a few minutes.

Ashwin was tired and frustrated, alright. Tahir got that. Anyone would be. After all, Prime Minister or not, at the end of the day, he was a human like everyone else!

♌

Ashwin was attending a meeting in a large conference room at the PMO. The darkness of the room was sleep-inducing; Ashwin felt effects of exhaustion as his entire body ached. The meeting was done halfway when Vidhan leaned over and told Ashwin that Naqvi wanted to meet him immediately.

Ashwin excused himself.

"What happened?" Ashwin asked the moment he entered the room.

"Well, the man exists. His plan for global destruction exists." Tahir replied.

"Oh? I am relieved it's not planted by GATC," Ashwin said sitting on his chair.

"Yes, which means that the evidence on nuclear weapon raw trading was real. But then, we couldn't find the weapon because it does not exist!"

"I'm confused!"

"Those deals for nuclear weapons were only to misguide us!" Tahir said nervously. "The man is a maniac! He knew the only thing which can catch undivided attention of this level is a nuclear threat!"

"So he traded material for a nuclear weapon just to misguide us? There is another agenda behind everything?" Ashwin asked.

"Yes, sir." Tahir gulped. "He made an even deadlier weapon."

"What?" Ashwin jolted up.

"A bio weapon developed in some banal lab at a harmless location has the capacity to affect over 75% of the world population, directly or indirectly. The mastermind has established connection with us and affirmed the information."

"Established connection? How?"

"Virtually."

"Did he say what he wants?"

"Nothing as of now."

"Outrageous! How do you know this is not another wild goose chase?"

"Let us hope not. We have tracked down a lead, who, we think, is directly linked to the mastermind."

♌

Rane threw his cigarette and moved out of the shadows. Shivankar Rane, field officer RAW, was following a lead that could connect them to the mastermind planning the biggest terrorist attack.

His target took an abrupt turn into one of the many alleys and Rane took the same route. He was not familiar with San Salvador, especially this part of the city, so he couldn't take an alternate route. His man began walking so swiftly that Rane had to suddenly end his conversation with an old lady, with whom he was speaking to make the pursuit discreet.

"*Damn*. He knows," Rane said, almost running behind the target.

Rane had to act fast. He checked his left pocket and felt his weapon. Soon the bullets would hit the kneecap of his target and Rane would round him up. A small girl was peeping from a window of one of the houses and Rane waved at her. He ensured to move out of that girl's sight at the time of fire. After he was away, he pulled out his automatic and was about to fire when a group of thirty odd drummers came out from a small street and began walking while beating the drums. His target was lost among them.

The Batucada procession.

Rane followed the drummers along with the rhythmically moving crowd. He could see his target again. He had changed into a yellow polo shirt similar to that of the bateria and was shaking a chocalho. Rane smiled; his target was good.

Rane's looks and command over Spanish helped him blend in. He too joined the procession like a local having a good time.

One tourist was having a good time as well. He was stopping frequently and taking pictures.

♌

Zahan slipped away from the bateria quietly, when they were playing the final beats. The final rhythms are normally magnanimous in beats and performances, as the bateria push hard to entertain the crowd. You can never come out from that madness which lasts for a little over one minute.

One minute was all Zahan needed to lose Rane.

He threw his chocalho near a small street and entered it. He looked on either side and felt relieved. He had been traced and he didn't have much time left. He took out a phone and made a call.

"Action. Now!" he spoke quickly and disconnected.

He immediately opened the back of his phone and was about to remove the SIM to destroy it, when a tourist in a blue linen shirt approached him. He looked confused.

"You speak English?" he asked moving closer.

"*Qué?*" Zahan replied in Spanish.

"I thought I heard you talking in English," said the tourist. He was holding a tablet, which he forwarded to Zahan.

"Umm, Inglés? No good!" Zahan replied quickly.

"Yeah I know," Dylan Bucklaw, the CIA agent for Central America, said as he pulled out a needle and injected it behind Zahan's ear. Zahan felt short of breath due to the sudden pain. He realized that his assaulter had been following his *bateria*, like an enthusiastic tourist. Zahan began falling. He remembered his SIM was still in the socket. He wanted to throw his device but his hands were paralysed. He saw Rane entering the alley. The last thing he remembered was being forcibly pushed into the backseat of a car.

♌

Dylan and Rane sat on a shaky table. They were inside a room in a cheap hotel; their prisoner was strapped to the bed. He would remain unconscious for at least eight hours.

Dylan opened his system and inserted the SIM. Zahan had made a call and they could trace the location of the receiver. They were a step closer to the mastermind. They both sat in front of that device for three hours. There were levels of insulation at the receiving end, but when they got the exact location, they almost tripped from their chairs.

"Damn!" Dylan said and made a call to DoS. Rane called NSA hoping it wasn't too late!

The attendance in GATC conference room was low. There were only six people – Chris, Anna, Ashwin, Jahvn, Manuha and Escrow. The presidents of France and China couldn't attend the meeting because of some urgent issues in their respective countries.

It wasn't comforting; there was deadly silence in the room now that the expected impact of the attack was wider.

"If at all we live to see a better world, the first thing we should ask GATC to do, is to change the interiors of their rooms. They all are bleak and depressing!" Chris said, when Manuha and Escrow went out for an update.

"Paint it red, eh?" asked Jahvn looking up from his device.

"Never give a communist your paint job," Chris smiled. "Red is the only colour they know."

Anna smiled as she looked up.

"Red is a powerful colour! I can prove it both metaphorically and scientifically," Jahvn replied. "I am a science graduate, you know, from the Moscow Institute of Physics and Technology State University and have a Ph.D. from Lomonosov Moscow State University."

"Showing off, are we?" Chris sneered.

"You can't match it up. Can you?" Fedyorov smiled.

"I don't need to. I chose vocational education. What's the difference?"

"The reds and the greens."

Ashwin put the stylus on the table and looked up. The conversation had become interesting.

"What difference does it make?" Anna quipped. "When you both are being bullied by someone who could be an illiterate!"

"Seriously. That's an insult to an injury. How can we let this happen?" Chris spoke. "I am appalled to think that a terrorist group, *not a country,* but a terrorist group rose to such power?"

"If you ask me, they always had an upper hand. Unlike us, they are not bound by the law." Ashwin said rubbing his chin. "Nobody controls them. No treaty, no UN, nothing. Besides people who join them, they are extremists of the same league. When they decide to destroy the world, they do it. There are no ifs and buts, neither for the leaders nor the followers."

"I agree. But somebody must be supporting them? Some country?" Chris asked.

"We can't say that for sure, unless we sit for negotiations. But I want to believe that it's not backed by a government."

They all wanted to believe that. All doubts on the legitimacy of the threat had been clarified after the terrorist established contact with GATC. It all started with an online video. In a seven-minute-long video, a nondescript man had pressed a very small piston at a park in Seoul; his actions remained unnoticed till him and people walking nearby, fell to the ground. They were rushed to the hospital and in less than forty-eight hours, they were dead.

Initially the incident looked harmless. Dehydrated joggers do pass out sometimes, but after that video was posted online, it created widespread panic in South Korea. It is only when South Korean police started investigating that they realized that the threat was anything, but local. In the small house of the man who pressed the piston, they found another CD with an AV file. A man, speaking in pitch darkness, confirmed his intent of mass destruction at a global scale.

That was when GATC jumped into action.

Manuha and Escrow returned with Dr McLain, Principal scientist for GATC. They all looked tense. Manuha swiped the screen and showed the image of world map with red dots scattered all over it.

"These red dots signify place of disarmament and the area it will affect!" Manuha said pointing at the image, "One dot has the capacity to affect a radius of seven thousand kilometres."

"So these are the locations mentioned in the CD?" Anna asked.

"Yes.We are expecting more," Manuha paused and then continued. "If the man *has* what he claimed to have for real, within two days, a large section of the global population will die."

"Within two days?" Anna asked anxiously. "Which type of bio weapon is that?"

Escrow introduced Dr McLain to the group and asked him to explain.

McLain got up from his seat and clicked on his system image of an angular structure appeared. "This is the virus strain which has been found in the body of all those who died in Korea.This is a genetically modified strain transmitted orally to the host body. After reaching the central circulation, this virus multiplies rapidly and redistributes itself to one of the vital organs, where it grows at greater affinity, stopping the function of that organ in no time.We are suspecting there is a chemical in the DNA of that virus, which impairs the immune system of the host.The blood acts as super culture media; in forty-eight hours, all the other body organs stop functioning and the victim dies.The effects of the viral infection start showing only after a few hours. It would have seemed like a case of heart attack, and remained completely unnoticed, had the terrorist not shared the video."

"Err... I guess if three or four people collapse at the same time, it will call for attention," Chris interjected. "And in the video, we can see that the virus infected the victim immediately."

"About that," McLain cleared his throat. "It wasn't the virus, which made people unconscious, but a compound that was released along with it," he gulped. "The master terrorist only did that to create a melodramatic effect; also to make his life easy, otherwise the victims would have been admitted to different hospitals. I am just saying, we are dealing with a lunatic here."

"What measures do we take?" Anna exclaimed. "We can't just sit here and watch. It won't be long when angry people will come out on streets demanding answers. For how long do you plan to cover it up?"

"Ma'am, it will only add to the chaos. Let us not rush and wait for the negotiations," Escrow said quietly.

"How long will it take for our scientists to come back with an antidote," Ashwin asked anxiously.

"We don't know, sir!' Escrow said empathetically. "Even as we are speaking the scientists are looking for quick measures to counter it. Let's hope the terrorist doesn't press the button before that."

"Any news from the field yet?" Chris asked shuddering at the thought of millions of dead people across the globe.

"No. They were supposed to contact us now. I must go and check," Escrow said and left.

"Please remove this image. It's not comforting to look at the weapon, which might kill you," Anna smiled trying to ease the suffocating silence.

"I understand!" Manuha touched the screen and the GATC insignia appeared.

"Only sometime back, we were discussing about changing the things inside."

"I am sorry?" Manuha asked looking confused.

"We thought GATC should make this place more vibrant." Anna smiled. "It will be less depressing that way."

"I understand," said Manuha standing up. "We may do it!"

"Glad you understood our desperate need for colour. Our lives have become so bleak." Anna smiled.

Manuha smiled back as he pressed a button under his table. A part of the table fell loose. He took out an automatic concealed there, snapped it into position and fired!

He saw all the bodies lying motionless on the floor. He wanted to confirm, but it was too late. He heard the click of the door, and before anybody could enter, he snapped out his cufflinks and swallowed them. The synthetic cyanide poison in that cufflink would kill him in seconds.

$$\text{\textOmega}$$

Tahir banged his fist on the wall as he entered the GATC conference room. All the four leaders and Dr McLain were lying lifeless on the floor. Manuha lay at the far end of the room, his eyes were wide and his mouth was frothing.

Only if they had been a few minutes early. Only if they had been a little more cautious.

Naqvi felt ashamed. The world had lost four strong leaders. Suddenly somebody called out from behind, "Mr Jamwal and Ms Svenson are still breathing."

He rushed to see them.

Thirty minutes later, on his way to the hospital, Naqvi received a text, which sent a chill down his spine.

Yi Jifang, the Chinese President and Alexei Lubont, the French President, had died in separate accidents. Alexei was assassinated, while Jifang's plane crashed in Nanjing.

$\mathbf{2}$

Brendon Hewitt, the UN Secretary General, buried his face in his hands. He was on a telephonic conference with all the major countries in the world. The terrorist had asked for one leader for negotiations and they were deliberating on the same.

Soon after the killing of leaders, GATC received an AV from the terrorist through Manuha's system. It was just the same as the one they had received earlier after the Seoul attacks. A man's voice over pitch darkness. This man took responsibility for the killings of all the leaders working with GATC. And just to assert his control he shared another video covering two attacks in the city of Nice and Osaka. A similar modus operandi was adopted, as that in the Seoul park. However, this time, the number of people affected was much higher – five hundred in Osaka stadium, and three hundred and seventy-five at a mall in Nice. The terrorist had asked for a conversation with one leader of a country, for negotiations, after twenty-four hours.

Escrow suggested Ashwin Jamwal. Nobody agreed.

On his big TV screen, Hewitt saw clippings from various countries; the people were out on the streets. They were enraged and scared at the same time. Not only had two terror attacks happened simultaneously, but also the top global leaders had been killed. There was news of peaceful processions, and news of riots and protests. There was news of people killing each other and news of suicides.

Hewitt knew they had to act fast, but they had reached a deadlock. The countries were not agreeing on one name. There was paranoia among leaders; they were worried that security and economy of their nations might be compromised. They knew they were dealing with a powerful enemy and nobody wanted to give control to someone else.

The meeting was not going anywhere and they were losing time.

Hewitt heard the Italian Prime Minister, "Ashwin is still in the hospital. I don't think he is fit enough—" another excuse.

It would go on this way, so Brendon interjected and said, "Of all the leaders who were part of the GATC mission, only the US President and the Indian PM survived. Ms Svenson is in a coma and it's highly unlikely that she will come to soon, hence it has to be the Indian Prime Minister." Leaders expressed their displeasure and for a few minutes the meeting was at a standstill, again. "We don't have time. Mr Jamwal is our only bet," he added, finally.

Ashwin was still dazed due to painkillers that had been injected in his veins. He has woken up an hour back in a London hospital, only to be told that he would be the person negotiating with the terrorist. Escrow and Tahir updated him about all the events after the GATC attack. He was lucky tohave survived; he had been hit thrice, but none of the bullets had damaged his vital organs. Ashwin didn't feel that ecstatic though. No Objection Certificates and Cooperation Agreements from more than a hundred countries of the world were lying on his bed; he may have to make some immediate decisions considering the wellbeing of the global population. He had been given a huge responsibility and he had no clue how to go about it.

He was about to negotiate with someone who had carried out one of the biggest political attacks in modern times and who had a weapon with the capacity to wipe off the entire population.

He would communicate with the terrorist through an interactive screen, hoisted on an adjustable rod, clamped to the edge of his bed. Leaders from UNSC member countries, the IMF chief, and the UN General Secretary would join the conference virtually from their respective locations. However, they would not communicate directly with the terrorist.

The FSB chief, CIA Director and Tahir were present in his room. An IT backend station was set up in the adjoining room. The bleak hospital room has been transformed into a state of the art office. They were all geared up to meet the terrorist.

The conference was to start in a few minutes. Ashwin looked blankly at the screen; the bottom screen had seven 2X2 insets with other participants of the conference.

"Am I live too?" Ashwin asked.

"You will be as soon as the conference starts," Tahir replied checking the interactive device once again. He motioned the make-up artist giving Ashwin a final touch up to leave. It was time.

The machine buzzed and all the chiefs stiffened in their seats. Tahir gave Ashwin thumbs up.

Ashwin touched the answer button and a screen came to life. It was dark.

"Oh, so you have been chosen to represent all the nations?" a male voice spoke from the darkness. "Why I am not surprised?"

"Who are you?" Ashwin asked anxiously.

"A man who brought you guys down to your to knees!" He paused. "We can waste time and exchange pleasantries, or we can talk."

"What do you want?"

"As I said, I just want to bring you guys down to your knees. That's it. I want control," the voice laughed menacingly.

"Aren't we already?" Ashwin replied.

"Not yet," the voice laughed softly. "First you tell me which currency has the highest value in the world?"

"What?" Ashwin asked, confused.

The voice repeated the question.

"I don't know. Dinar? KWD?" Ashwin squinted.

"And lowest?"

"I don't know!" Ashwin replied firmly, "What is this, some kind of a quiz show?"

"You wish!" replied the man. "Before I ask more questions and humiliate you, let me tell you that I have sent my men all over the globe. They all look like normal people roaming around in the busiest streets, with one difference – they have small vials containing the virus strain.

"I like to call them Messengers of Death. Cool, isn't it? It's funny because it's true." The man laughed. "Those men are sadists. They have lost their families, they have been betrayed by their own country, and they have nothing to lose. They will not think twice before opening the vial."

"We know this and that's why I am here. Thousands of people are at risk."

"Thousands?" The man laughed. "Let me calculate it for you… umm…so many…. Multiply…umm number of cities…" he mumbled before saying, "Well the estimate comes to fifty…no five hundred! Yes, five hundred million. That would be the first round. I will kill as many every day and you will just watch helplessly!" he added menacingly.

"What do you want?" Ashwin asked beginning to sweat.

"Now we are talking! The figures always do the trick. First let me tell you, you were right about the most valued currency! You win nothing though!" He laughed. "The lowest right now is Iranian Riyal."

"Okay!"

"I want you to make Iranian Riyal the *only* petro currency."

"What?" Ashwin asked confused.

"Make Riyal the only currency for petro trading. What are not you getting?" the man said irritated.

"But, that's crazy! It will affect the global economy," Ashwin said angrily. The FSB chief Mikhail Namtriovic got up. He motioned Ashwin to calm down and not react. Since they were tracking the IP location of the terrorist, Ashwin was supposed to drag on the conversation,

"I am not done yet!" the man said firmly, "I also want you to make crude the 'only' usable source of energy!"

"That's outrageous!" Ashwin couldn't control his anger. "Many economies will fail as the balance of power will be shifted," Ashwin said only realizing that that was what the terrorist wanted. Major economies would topple if they agreed to the request. A new war of existence might start among the nations. It would take generations to recuperate from such a crisis. Damn!

"That's what I want!"

All the leaders were shaking their heads in the insets.

"It's crazy. I don't think we can do it!"

"What? Your posse refused, eh?" the terrorist said angrily. "I bloody asked for one person with control and they gave me a puppet. You are nothing but their mouthpiece. Filth! That's what I get!" he said disgusted.

"Say whatever. This is ridiculous. The outcome will be worse than both the world wars combined together. Before economies could settle, millions will be homeless. Many will die either starvation or in wars. People will suffer for generations."

"They will die anyway; either from the monetary crisis or from my virus," he paused and then added thinking. "I can't believe you just said no!" He sounded surprised. "Hello? I am the one who managed to kill five powerful leaders of the world in the world's most sterile office. I am the one who killed people in Osaka and Nice and I am the one with the weapon!" He yelled like a maniac. *"So when I give orders, I want action!"*

He then added pleasantly, "And I want you to get this done in five hours."

"What?" Ashwin said angrily, agitated with the histrionics. "These things do not happen with the snap of a finger."

He looked at Mikhail who was asking him to lower his tone. He expelled his breath and said, "Considering your undisputed knowledge of the global economy and politics, I am sure you know that there is a process to do something as drastic as what you have proposed."

"Massaging my ego, eh?" The man chuckled. "An old, yet effective technique! But I am impressed that the Indian PM is resorting to such measures," he laughed. "They've given you instructions, right? Ask for time, understand his psyche, and make him talk. Do not get angry. I know these things from the good old days. I am impressed; they've trained you well!"

"I got up only an hour back!" Ashwin replied sharply. "I have not received any training. The bullets you misfired immobilized me for nearly a day! I thought you would know, it's not possible to do it in five hours. Even with all the technology, we need time."

"We do not misfire, Mr Jamwal, and we don't do things unplanned. I knew you'd ask for more, so tell me how much time you need?"

"Four or five business days," Ashwin said after a while. The IMF chief was showing all his ten fingers, signifying ten days, *or months?* He didn't know. Ashwin knew that the terrorist had purposely given five hours; they would not get anything over twenty-four hours.

"You get twelve hours."

"It's impossible! You know that! I will patch you with the IMF chief. You could talk to him."

"Fuck the process!" the man replied angrily. "I will make it five hours and you can do nothing about it!"

"I can say no," Ashwin said with finality. "We don't have to be pushed by you; we will evaluate the damage. It's not a game—"

"You still can't give up on your instincts. Can you? You all just can't give up control," The man interjected Ashwin.

"And let people like you have it?" Ashwin said under his breath. "Running amok with the deadliest weapon and threatening to destroy the entire human race?"

"Yet, we are no different," the man added calmly. "You too have weapons. There are treaties restricting your usage of deadly weapons, still you develop a deadlier one almost every year. We both are killers of the same league, except that you justify your killing by calling it political."

"No! We don't kill innocent people and we don't kill people without any reason."

The man laughed. There was no truth in what Ashwin had just said.

"This lying comes naturally with the profession, doesn't it?" the man spoke. "Innocents are not killed by you? Tell that to the grieving mother in Iraq, or brother of a rape victim in China. You *bloody* do everything under the sun in the name of politics and then call us terrorists?"

"So this is revenge?" Ashwin asked

"No! I took my revenge in the GATC London office," the man slightly leaned forward and the glow of his monitor showed his chin – a white man.

"Mr Jamwal, we don't have time. You only have twelve hours. All my people are carrying a virucidal chemical which will destroy the virus, if you do as you are told. If you don't or if you try to harm me, my messengers will deliver their message, so hurry…chop chop!"

He went offline.

Ashwin had never felt so exhausted in his life. He swiped the screen and all insets changed into larger boxes. Everyone looked tense.

"We can't let this happen. We just can't!" Javier Vacario, Vice President of the US was the first one to speak. "That man is maniac. We will only make him more powerful!"

"We don't have a choice!" said Brendon Hewitt tiredly. "We have to follow his orders. Even if we find and kill him within twelve hours, his men will open the vials."

"What if he is fibbing?" Javier asked.

"What if he is not?" Hewitt said exasperatedly.

"We don't know that. And what if there are no Messengers of Death? He is just a maniac," said Cyril Bach, the ad-hoc UK Prime Minister. "I think we should wait and not act."

"And jeopardize the lives of millions of innocent people?" Hewitt asked, shaking his head.

"But if we follow his demands, we are putting billions of lives at stake!" Javier pressed.

"But they will live! They will get a chance to work it out and it won't be long before it will all stabilize. There are chances for a small economy to become powerful. But we all will get to live."

"That's just a beautiful thought," said Javier again, "But it's not practical! We are talking about the greatest depression that might follow."

Nobody else spoke, so Hewitt got the hint. They all agreed with Javier.

"That sickens me," he said. "You all are worried only and only about losing control. You are least bothered about those people who could die after twelve hours! You don't even want to give them a chance to fight it out," he said in disgust.

"We should carry out his orders!" Ashwin said after thinking. "He is not backed by a country. He just wants to make us suffer. His animosity is with governments of the world and not the people. People are just the collateral damage. Those people have every right to live!"

"You are out of your mind!" Damien Baudin, the new French President said angrily. "We have to test the waters before jumping! We should wait!"

"And watch millions die? I want you to respect me when you have put me in charge!" Ashwin said looking briefly at Mikhail and the CIA director, Trystan M. Johanson. They nodded because they realized that Ashwin has something in his mind.

"Obviously we made a wrong choice!" Javier said bitterly. "You are taking unrealistic decisions!"

"It's not political, Mr Vacario," Hewitt said firmly, "but not unrealistic. In fact, Mr Jamwal's decision is more humane than what you all are proposing. Testing waters means death for millions. Five hundred million people, for god's sake."

Javier said something, but Ashwin couldn't hear him as the analyst from the next room rushed in. "Sir, we have traced the location of the caller!"

"Which is?" said Trystan moving towards him.

"Nattakom, Kottayam, Kerala. India!" the analyst read out the transcript.

Ashwin stopped breathing. Indian? Tahir went over and glanced at the transcript. It was unbelievable.

"Strange thing; this man has a foreign accent," the analyst said.

"Indians are voice trained for that," Tahir said looking at the sheet.

"Sir, we separated each word. One cannot be voice trained to have such impeccable pronunciation. That accent is definitely of a Russian."

Ivan Kuruserv.

♌

It was six in the morning and the hospital room bathed in the soft sunlight. Twelve hours had passed but nobody in that room had slept; they were all waiting for the call.

The monitor at Ashwin's bed buzzed. The screen went dark again

"We did it," Ashwin said wearily.

"Great! I know you would!" the voice beamed.

"Please ask your people to destroy the virus."

"Of course I will! Let me confirm first."

"Now! Please. By accepting your request I have compromised my country's position in the geopolitical arena! I went against everyone, because I wanted to give those people a chance to live and struggle, rather than die an unknown death."

"Neat!" the voice came back after some time." I have checked Tokyo Exchange. Wow! What great numbers, it's a plunge!" The man gave a guttural laugh. "I will call off my messengers!"

"Please do it in front of me!" Ashwin pressed.

"I hate taking orders from swine like you!" he said menacingly. "But it doesn't matter. You are nobody." The man then spoke to someone else." It's done! Call the party off."

"How do we know they have destroyed the virus?" Ashwin asked

"How? I don't know that myself. They should and if at all they decide not to, you can't control them. Nobody can!" he chuckled and then added, 'Now I can die peacefully. So Long."

♌

Ivan Kuruserv smiled. He leaned back on his wheelchair. His wrinkled face had peace after twenty years.

Yes, he could die peacefully now.

He closed his eyes and let his mind go to his parent's house. He saw Boris and himself playing in the snow as their mother called them for sweet pirog. Happy times! Suddenly he heard the click of a gun. He did not turn, as the intruder pressed the barrel on the back of his skull; he heard a gasp and then felt his nostrils burning with a strong acrid smell.

♌

Subin Jose, former field officer, RAW, looked at the insentient figure on the wheelchair and cringed with disgust. The man on a wheelchair, who threatened to bring an end to the world, looked close to death himself. He was an old man, in his seventies. His body was feeble, the veins on his arms were visible and he had scars and blisters all over his body.

Subin moved around the room and checked all the drawers and cupboards. He sorted stuff, kept those that were important, and left the rest. He then shuffled through the papers kept next to a huge system. He took whatever he felt was necessary and threw most of it in the garbage. He also tried to access the system, but couldn't get through. It took him exactly ten minutes to finish his search.

Subin sat on the edge of the bed, the only furniture in that room. He checked his watch. It was around noon. Twelve hours back he was planning to sleep peacefully after a long day in his new workplace.

Then he got an unexpected call from the NSA Tahir Naqvi.

In less than two hours, he was sent from Chennai to Kottayam. From there he took several modes of transport to reach Nattakom.

He covered the entire village by foot. It was dark and quiet. Occasionally street dogs chased him, but he managed to make the mental map of the entire village in less than an hour. He located the place, and crouched behind a small temple. He squinted and looked at the ordinary looking house, uphill. This was the house, which has the most dreaded terrorist of modern times. Unbelievable. Jose had to act fast; morning will break in an hour, exposing him.

He took out his thermal imager and adjusted its range and focus. He could see a number of people in the house. He saw the heat contour in the room upstairs. It only had one person. The ground floor had three people. Then he took out another device to detect electromagnetic fields, helping him locate a camera or a sensor in that house. He found two cameras and three motion sensors. Then he waited.

Timing and precision was the key to this operation. He couldn't act a minute earlier or later than the designated time. Subin looked at his watch. He still had four hours; enough time to draft his strategy. He found spots to hide from the camera. Once that was done, Subin discarded his jacket, revealing a cheap T-shirt. He pressed the bell and entered.

A hefty man sat up straight; he had been sleeping on a cot in the garden.

"My pug has entered your house. I am sorry I need to find him; his name is Buzo." Jose said in Malayalam and moved to the position where the cameras could not find him. He then called out Buzo several times.

"No pup came here!" that man roared, getting up from his position.

"I said *pug* and he did!" Jose crouched for a while. "He is very small! I only came here today to visit my aunt. I took him out for a walk when he—"

"There is no dog here! Get out of this property," the man said coming forward.

"Please understand, he is like family! He definitely entered this house, through that gap between gates." Jose pointed at the space. "I am not leaving without him"

"Well, then I have to throw you out!" The man reached for Subin's collar. That's what Jose wanted! He turned and hit the man behind the skull. He began falling. Jose caught him and dragged him away from the camera's vision.

Another man appeared at the doorway.

"Sriju?" He must have heard the commotion. He noticed Jose and was about to reach for a gun, when Subin fired. He died instantly.

Carefully, Subin entered the house; preparing himself for another attack but there wasn't any. Some noises were coming from the last room; he slowly opened it and found a man sleeping on a chair. Highlights of an old cricket match was running on the TV. Subin took out a small plastic bottle and shook it. He opened the door again, threw the bottle and closed it immediately. He waited for five minutes before entering the room. The man was still on chair, but he was unconscious. Jose locked him in the room and went upstairs. He hid behind the walls and waited for the conversation to end. Then he moved in and knocked out the master manipulator – a crippled septuagenarian.

♌

Subin shook his head. He sighed, got up from the bed and made a call.

"Mission accomplished."

♌

Ashwin Jamwal disconnected the call and made another one. After confirmation, that Kuruserv did not have any aides and he in fact, was the mastermind behind the attacks, the IMF chief rescinded the earlier orders. Confused investors were cynical and markets remained bearish for some time. But as the day matured, the chronology of the events flashed on every news channel. So much had happened; from the killing of top leaders, to attacks in Osaka and Nice, followed by a temporary upheaval in the global economy. Markets would not bounce back immediately, transactions would be slow for a few weeks, but gradually it would normalize. There was hope and Ashwin Jamwal was the reason behind it.

♌

Ashwin picked up his coffee as he disconnected the phone. It was his eighth cup. He looked at the people sitting in his room.

"Mr Hewitt just released his comments," Trystan said reading out from his tablet.

"The world owes a great deal to a team of very determined leaders, and above all, Ashwin Jamwal," he smiled and raised his cup as a mark of honour.

Ashwin smiled back; there was nothing like the feeling of accomplishment.

Trystan continued, "Countries joining hands…blah blah, more praises for Mr Jamwal…countries have set up examples…blah blah, another round of praise for Mr Jamwal, more moral lessons…World peace!" Everybody laughed at his act.

"Seriously, sir, I marvel at this man's brilliance. He made leaders of the world work together!" he added finally.

"I don't know whether to be happy or sad about this remark," Ashwin took a sip. "By the way, when will you start the interrogations? Let's be very sure that he doesn't have an accomplice with more weapons."

"We will make sure," Trystan replied pleasantly. "Ivan will be flown to Gitmo tomorrow and after one week to Lubyanka. He will be detained in Lubyanka since he has a Russian passport."

"Gitmo?" Ashwin raised his eyebrows.

"Don't worry sir. Unlike what people think, we are not inhumane to detainees," Trystan replied getting up.

"I will show you some reports of your 'humane' treatment," Mikhail said smiling. "We are clearly not on the same page on the subject of humanity."

"When the heads of CIA and FSB start bickering, we can say the world has gone back to normal!" Ashwin joked and everybody laughed.

After a while, everybody left, except for Tahir, who could not keep the smile off his face. Technically, it was 'his' man, who had wrapped up the mission.

"I can't be happier," Tahir said and then after noticing discomfort on Ashwin's face he added, "You look worried."

"Aren't we celebrating a little too early?" Ashwin said, keeping his cup on the table. "How can we be sure that the virus is not out there?"

"We have confirmed from his system that he doesn't have allies. We haven't heard of a single causality till now," Tahir replied. "If we think that way, we are always exposed to such attacks. Even as we are speaking, somebody may be developing a deadlier weapon. We can't control that."

"So this man gone, another will rise in power? Where do we stand? Under the guns?"

"Sadly, yes." Tahir replied grimly. "But we have learned our lesson sir. We will be more cautious. We will find ways to counter such attacks. We will become stronger; politically and otherwise."

"Still, I am not convinced."

"It's unnecessary paranoia, sir," Tahir said.

"I hope it is," Ashwin shook his head. "Though I still feel we could trace him only because he wanted to be traced."

"What?"

"We had this feeling earlier as well," Ashwin frowned. "A man so well insulated, cannot be traced in one day. Don't you find it odd that the mastermind of such a great plan would hide in Nattakom, protected only by three guards? You are sure he doesn't have a boss?"

"Ninety-nine percent, sir! These people are overconfident. That's what destroys them,"Tahir replied, though he was troubled by the new fact. "That man was Russian, so he never thought he could be traced in India!"

There was a knock at the door and Adya peeped in. Ashwin nodded, so she walked in but stopped as she saw the NSA standing in the corner.

"Oh! I am sorry…I thought I could see you now," she said uncomfortably to Ashwin.

"Don't worry. We are not discussing anything classified."

Tahir watched Adya taking a seat and said, "Sir, I think you should rest now!" With that he left.

"That's true." Adya said holding his hands. "After all, you have saved the world."

"Oh! That's what is trending?" Ashwin smiled.

"Not exactly! We have been allowed limited coverage. It's heavily edited, but in the end, you get all the credit," she smiled. "I am just glad to see you alive—"

"I am alive because I was meant to be," Ashwin said uneasily. "There were no misfires." Adya looked at him confused.

"There is something wrong." Ashwin shook his head.

"Nothing that should concern you, now," Adya said pressing the button and reclining the bed. "Rest now."

"Maybe when they interrogate him, they will find out!" Ashwin said lying down.

"You rest as you won't get enough rest for a few days; there are many people lined up to meet you." Adya said stroking his hair

"Who?"

"The press, diplomats, international committee heads, etcetera! It's very difficult to get past the security. They have even stalled Javier Vacario, Vice President of the US."

"Oh? Then how did you get in?" Ashwin asked though he knew she was exaggerating.

"I said I am his special someone!"

Part-III

He who knows the summit of the intelligence of the ashva (horse), becomes illumined and fit for the sacrifice.

—Yajur Veda, Taittiriya Samhita, Khand VII. 5. 25

Hades

I am a sufferer. I know what pain is. The excruciating physical pain and enduring pain of being what you are. It's hard to live through that pain. I lived it. But it won't be like this for long. It will end....

When did it start? I don't know. Have I tried getting rid of it? Many times. Did I succeed? Not like I wanted. The memories keep coming back, making it more difficult. I wanted to get out of it...the pain.

I have to find a mission. I have to think it all through. My aspirations are for myself, but I can't do it alone. I made a plan. I made a team.

Ashwin Jamwal

I just wanted to be the ruler of the world. You have to de-throne a powerful man to be the most powerful. The ironies of the world. I was itching to defeat the single most powerful person and there wasn't any. I was left with only one choice – To create a powerful person.

I don't know when I stumbled upon Ashwin Jamwal. He might even have failed to make a significant impression at first. Slowly, I saw a leader in him. I saw unease in him. I saw he had the desire to make a difference. I saw all the qualities in him that I want to see in a powerful leader. The only problem was that he doesn't seem keen to become powerful. Only God knows how much I had to sweat to make this a reality.

A.K. Nandi and his woman, Sumona

He helped me many times. In fact, I was starting to like him so much that I made him my plan B. He had all the qualities of a powerful leader, except one – he was far too cunning for my taste.

And also, I felt he somehow came to know of my true identity. I guess he heard me or had his people snoop. I couldn't take chances. I had to kill him. Jawahar, whose daughter Nandi had raped, left no stone unturned to give him a slow and painful death.

On the brighter side, I learned to become more cautious from that day.

Sumona died for the same reason. I couldn't take chances. That old pig was far too involved with Sumona. He could have shared my identity. She also died because I needed money.

Zahan

Zahan was my most trusted employee of all. He had seen the worst of hell. I met him in Ahlat, Turkey. He was a young boy full of rage. Originally from Afghanistan, that boy had seen his father stoned to death. His mother revolted and was later killed. Her dead body remained on the street for days till the hawks pecked all her flesh.

"I was given a stone to throw at my father," he told me. "I was six. I don't think my stone reached him. But I actually hurled one at my father. I sat in the dust and saw my mother's body getting pierced by birds. I was molested by my own uncles. It seems there is some sexual pleasure in seeing an eight-year-old cry when a rusted iron rod is inserted in his anus."

He was the victim of an unfair system. When he was ten, he was adopted by some distant relatives in Scotland. They managed to give him a better life, but they couldn't erase those dreadful memories. Zahan, like me, hated his life and like me, was looking for avenues to escape it. I gave him a cause to believe in.

He had seen me. He believed me.

Zahan was my right arm. He managed everything under my name in my absence. He had never disappointed me. He chose to appear before RAW just so they could locate me.

Zahan would always remain my son.

Manuha

Another victim of cruelty; his pains were buried deep until I scratched them open. He asked me, "How do you know of my pain?"

I told him I saw it in his eyes. But I had actually found about him through Kuruserv. We needed a big shot in global security. We got Manuha.

Kuruserv

I saw him mourning his brother's death. He was travelling all across the globe to heal the pain and I happened to see him in Delhi. Kuruserv made my team complete. He may have become old, his body coordination may have rusted, his legs may have been paralysed completely, but what didn't fade were his sharpness and his intent to avenge his brother's death.

He loathed the system, like no other. Given a chance, he could have blown up the entire earth by himself. He was a sadist, but he was unaligned; I gave him a path to follow.

It took me almost twenty-five years to get my plan ready. I have worked hard for this day.

Whatever I did, I did for this day.

Now the time has come to reveal the most powerful man on earth.

$\unicode{2658}$

Tahir flipped through TIME magazine, while waiting anxiously for Ashwin to come out of an important meeting. TIME magazine had named Ashwin Jamwal the person of the year.

Almost an year had passed since the terrorist threat; Ashwin Jamwal has become a household name across the globe. While people of the world owed him greatly for saving their lives, global organizations began seeing India in a different perspective altogether. Call it a trust factor, India could now voice its opinion in global issues. India's geopolitical position had improved, and from being just a bridging nation, India became a power centre. Ashwin Jamwal became the most powerful man in the world, that's what Forbes said.

"I am sorry, Naqvi. The meeting went on longer than expected," Ashwin said entering in the office. "We are trying to close SEZ trade agreement with Japan."

"You're busier than before. I thought you'd take things a little easy after that event…" Tahir replied smiling. "We all did."

"You know I took a break! I was away for two weeks. That's a lot in Prime Minister years." Ashwin laughed.

"I know about that vacation. You were too reckless about security for my liking."

"I don't see my parents much. They refused to come to Delhi and I cannot go to Allahabad. They are very private people so that holiday was much required." Ashwin smiled. "It is good to get away from the continuous security and political ruckus. Once in a while"

"I would still say you needed more security than you had."

"I am fine and that's what should matter! So what's the news?"

"I don't have good news! Ivan Kuruserv died in the morning today."

"During interrogation?"

"Well, not exactly. Kuruserv was already close to death when we caught him. He spent more time in a hospital than in an interrogation room."

"But who is going to explain that to human right activists in Geneva?" Ashwin shook his head. "Did you get anything from him?"

"Nothing, except about the lab which manufactured that virus."

"I know. You told me that. Nothing about why he did it?"

"No, sir!" Tahir replied uneasily, "but the man we got at El Salvador told us something we had ignored, until Ms Batra called today—"

"Adya?" Ashwin said in shock. "What?"

"That man from El Sal spoke of a name – Hades. Till this morning we had presumed it to be one of Ivan Kuruserv's many names, but then Hades contacted Ms Batra."

"What? We were celebrating too early. I knew it! Who is this Hades?"

"We don't know. Ms Batra is coming over. She has something to show us."

♌

Tahir diligently inserted a small storage device into the socket of his system. He was with Adya in a secure conference room. Adya requested the NSA for complete confidentiality on the matter. He agreed to look at the content first, to be able to decide accordingly.

Tahir's heartbeat stopped the moment the screen went blank and a hoarse male voice filled the small conference room.

"The power of power cannot be gauged. It exists more strongly than other forces of nature. I am Hades and I desire to be the most powerful man on earth." The man spoke with dramatic voice modulation. "But then how to become one, especially in the current scenario? Alexander once said: Heaven cannot brook two suns, nor earth two masters. But now the earth has so many masters: there are ones who are politically strong working in daylight, and then there are others who operate in the dark. All are equally controlling. In short, there are far too many masters. If I am taking either of the paths – to be politically strong or to be criminally strong – I'll only end up being one in the crowd. I don't want that. I want exclusive control. But for that, I have to eliminate all the existing powers! Powers? Can you believe it is plural? You have powerful industrialists, powerful leaders, technocrats, mafia, radicals and what not. Is it too much to ask for one powerful person, *just one*? Apparently it is! I can't go on defeating a hundred so called powerful people in different sectors, so I had to create one single most powerful person just so I can defeat him or her and become one myself. He laughed softly and continued. "It took me years to do so, but I planned. I never deterred and finally I have someone, who is not only politically strong but has successfully overpowered, presumably the most dreadful criminal of the modern era," he paused and added. "I made Ashwin Jamwal."

Tahir almost fell off his chair.

"Who could have thought that an Indian PM would ever top the list of the most powerful men on earth, but he did. He now has the power to even dictate world leaders. But everything, every bit in Ashwin's life was regimented, controlled by me. He became what he is today, because I wanted him to – *The Ashwin Jamwal*."

He paused again to let the story sink in.

"Now the time has come for him to have a rendezvous with his creator. Now the time has come for the creator to destroy his masterpiece and make place for a new one. Bigger and better." He laughed menacingly.

"Ashwin Jamwal, I will meet you on the 9th of August 2021. It's an important date. Where and when? I'll let you find that out!"

The audio stopped and for a few minutes the only sound in that room was the buzz from the projector.

Tahir threw an ashtray at the screen. "Damn!"

♞

"This is crazy!" Ashwin shook his head after watching the video. "How can somebody claim to make me do things I always wanted to do? It's a scam! I worked hard all my life and then a man appears from nowhere and says that he's made me. Unbelievable," he said shifting his gaze from Adya to Tahir.

"Everything I have done so far was planned by someone else? How silly does that sound?"

"Silly as it may seem, we have no choice but to believe that man's threat," Tahir replied cautiously. "You remember you said that the events around WMD didn't make sense and something was missing? I guess *this* was the real agenda."

"What are you saying?" Ashwin frowned. "This Hades controlled the events around WMD threat so that I could become the most powerful man?"

Nobody replied.

Ashwin thought a while and added, "But now it seems possible. Manuha must have convinced members of the GATC and Security General to include India in that meeting. Manuha worked for Hades!" Ashwin rubbed his face with his hands. "Which means I haven't worked hard. I haven't even been lucky. Things were made to happen for me. It's sad, but it's possible." Adya passed him a glass of water, but he refused and continued talking.

"Come to think of it, over ten PMs must have come before me, but no one could take India to the position where it is today. I could.

They were not incompetent. I am! I can't take credit for anything now. I am not worth anything! I am just a puppet."

Ashwin felt that he was going down in a swirl. Depression. It started coming back.

"Pull yourself together, Ashwin!" Adya said firmly after listening to Ashwin's self-contemplating tirade.

"There could be a possibility that Hades had facilitated events around you but he did not make Ashwin Jamwal what he really is today. People respect you not because they are forced to do so, but because they want to. So please stop pitying yourself. We don't have time for this."

"We have only four days. We need to act fast!" Tahir said urgently.

♌

"Is the 9th of August important to you?" Adya asked Ashwin. They were in the guest room of the PM's residence where Adya was staying.

"I don't know!" Ashwin said rubbing his forehead. "May be it's some random date?"

"I doubt. He said that it is an important date, and we think it is related to you. It could be anything: your first job, some important policy signing date, some date pertaining to your enemies. There are endless possibilities. Think hard. I will begin my own research and find out."

Ashwin got up and walked to the study table. "I am so restless now," he said taking out some pills and gulping them down with water. "It is disheartening to know that you have been manoeuvred. I am planning to quit from this post. I am not meant for it."

"Stop it Ashwin!" Adya said from behind. "You are one hell of a PM! How you became one is immaterial."

She may have rebuked him, but she felt sorry for Ashwin.

She looked at him; he was on the phone, asking someone to give him a few dossiers.

Dossiers! Ashwin's Dossier.

She got up, suddenly remembering a blue file which Aaron has given to her after resigning. That file, according to Aaron had some deep and dark information on Ashwin. That file had remained locked in her cabinet and Adya never got a chance to look at it thoroughly, but she had somehow remembered to bring it with her.

"What happened?" asked Ashwin alarmed at Adya's sudden movement.

"Nothing. Where is my bag?" she said looking around.

"I don't know." Ashwin shrugged.

Adya found it next to the couch.

"Your dossier!" Adya said taking out the blue file. "If it's an important date, related to you, we might find it here. You don't have to stress yourself."

"Okay." Ashwin sat next to her

Adya quickly skimmed through each page. It was a thorough report. It could have made an excellent coverage. It had everything – from Ashwin's school adventures, jobs, to his modus operandi... everything. Adya kept turning pages until she saw something and gasped.

"It's your birthday!" Adya said quietly.

"My birthday is on the 4th of February. You know that!" Ashwin frowned.

"No, the 4th of February is your adoption date. You were born on the 9th of August."

♌

Adya was about to call Ashwin's mother when Tahir entered.

"What happened?" Tahir asked taking his seat next to her. They were in PM's office in his residence. "I heard he is sick."

"He almost fainted yesterday after discovering that he was born on the 9th of August."

"He didn't know his birthday?"

"He didn't know he was adopted."

"Our man knows Mr Jamwal in and out!" Tahir said solemnly.

"I am scared. I will speak to his mother and find out more."

"Do that. We are short of time. I have asked Secretary Research and an IB FO to help us with this."

"Mr Naqvi!" Adya cried, "We talked about keeping it confidential."

"We don't have time. We need people," replied Tahir and left.

Adya dialled his mother's number.

"From where did you adopt Ashwin?" She asked after exchanging pleasantries with her

"Sri Mataji Trust, Indore," Mrs Jamwal replied simply. Adya expected her to be shocked, but the words came out flawlessly.

"Why didn't you tell Ashwin about his adoption?"

"We did." Mrs Jamwal sighed. "He just refused to believe it. Dear, Ashwin was seven when we adopted him. He knew it. He just never accepted it."

♌

Tahir finished de-briefing Intelligence Bureau's most trusted Field Officer Mrinal Verma.

"Way too dramatic and hard to believe," said Verma rolling his wrist.

"Yet every bit of it is possible," Tahir replied.

"This man is really sharp and we have to get him in less than three days' time," Shantanu Jha, Secretary Research added. "You up for it?"

"I am normally but—"

"Nothing is normal these days," Tahir said immediately. "Refer to this file for information on Mr Jamwal, " Tahir said passing the blue file to him.

"I have skimmed through it," Mrinal replied casually. "We can rule out the possibility that Hades is someone close because no one around Mr Jamwal looks competent enough to plot such a plan."

"Anyone could," replied Tahir. "All the dreadful criminals of the world are humble people in real life. Let's not forget that. Leave no stone unturned."

♌

"Please, can you look it up and let me now," Mrinal said with urgency in his voice. He was at the Sri Mataji Trust.

"It is difficult," the old female caretaker said between coughing. "It's a forty-year-old file."

"I know! But it's about a hefty ancestral property. My mother has lost the adoption papers. I need to have the details to present in the court tomorrow. If I don't find it, I will lose it all. Please understand," Mrinal pleaded.

"I understand. But our data maintenance is poor. I will still try," she said moving the cursor aimlessly on the screen. 'I can't promise anything though! I don't have a helper. We take care of over five hundred children. We don't have funds for basic necessities. Nobody cares for data maintenance."

"I will make a donation!" Mrinal added quickly.

"Let me check!" the lady's face beamed as she typed slowly on her keyboard. Mrinal felt that her indirect way was no better than asking for a bribe!

"I found something...but now I am confused," she said looking at the monitor.

"What happened?"

"You see, two Tamil kids were adopted by two families in Allahabad almost at the same time. I don't know which one is your brother."

"It's strange; I don't think many families from Allahabad would come to Indore to adopt."

"But it is all here. Two boys brought by the central trust from TN were adopted by families in Allahabad. One was eight years and the other seven. Both adopted on the 4th of February 1982. So which one is your brother?"

"I don't know. I wasn't even born then." Mrinal shrugged.

Two boys? He had to look at the system. In all likelihood, the other adopted kid is Hades.

"I will match your surname with the adoption parents. Then I will share the documents if I have any."

"Mahopatra," he replied, thinking of an uncommon surname in Allahabad.

"Mahopatra?" the lady shrieked. "There is no Mahopatra here! Are you sure your brother was adopted from this centre?"

"Definitely! I wouldn't have travelled from London if I was not sure. Let me have a look. Maybe they have only used their middle name. Maybe a friend of my parents adopted my brother first and then my parents adopted him!" Mrinal said leaning over to look at the system.

"See for yourself then!" the lady replied as she turned the screen.

Two families from Allahabad who adopted kids from this centre were Jamwal and Deb.

Arun Deb.

♌

It was one in the morning. Shantanu Jha, Secretary Research, was questioning Ashwin in front of Tahir and Adya. The process would have taken less time if Ashwin was not so disturbed. They had to frame each question very cautiously.

"Here in this file it's mentioned that Armugham played a major role in bringing you to politics and then making you a household name. Correct?" asked Shantanu.

Ashwin nodded. "There are many others!"

"Yes, if you could elaborate. We are going by Hades theory of creation, so we will try and find out who helped you in becoming what you are today and then zero down on one person."

"We already have that person!" Adya said angrily. "We have found the man! Mrinal gave his name but you are afraid to say it," she said looking at Tahir and Shantanu.

"Madam, please understand. We are going through a process," Jha replied. There was no process; he just didn't want to point out Arun's name. He wanted Ashwin to derive at the conclusion.

"We don't have time. Don't you get it? We have less than forty-eight hours now!"

"Who?" Ashwin asked confused. "Who is that person?"

"I don't find the need to go roundabout when we have found our man!" Adya said firmly.

"Who? Dammit!"

"Arun Deb!"

"What? You must be out of your mind," Ashwin said furiously.

"Read this report and then tell me. I have highlighted the content for your reference!"

Ashwin read it quietly.

"It doesn't make him Hades! Yes, he has helped me achieve my goals. He is a friend! That's what friends do!"

"Please read it properly, Ashwin," Adya said passing him the report again. "It clearly says that Arun has always worked, inconspicuously, to fulfil *your* aspirations. Who does that?"

"And see here," she pointed at the highlighted text and read from it, "Mrs Deb, in an interview mentioned, that at end of it all, Arun will come out stronger and more powerful."

Ashwin shook his head.

"It still doesn't prove a thing."

He asked Jha and the NSA pointing to the file, "Based on this, you are suspecting Arun?"

"No sir!" Tahir cleared his throat. "We have some other evidence which supports it. Like Mr Arun Deb had suffered from a mental disorder and had fits of violence and destruction. Soon after he was adopted, he was sent to a mental asylum for an year. It was found his mental illness was linked with subjugation. He was anti-authoritative. He wanted control. Had it not been for your mother, Mrs Deb would have never taken him back." Tahir said looking at Ashwin, who was sitting quietly.

"Such a person can never work for his best friend's aspirations to become a leader of any sort. Forget a global leader. Isn't it obvious now, Ashwin?" Adya asked.

Ashwin wasn't listening. His whole world was crashing before him. It was unbelievable. His best friend?

"Arun? Can he?" he spoke to himself.

"I am sorry, Ashwin," Adya said taking his face in her hands. "We need to end this madness. I can't see you like this."

"Nobody is touching Arun!" Ashwin said getting up. "I will call him right now!"

"No, sir!" Shantanu exclaimed loudly. "Please don't speak to him. We have called him here already. We will arrange for the rendezvous."

"Your call could be disastrous to both Mr Deb and yourself. We will find more evidence before doing anything. Trust us," said Tahir getting up.

Too late to make promises.

♌

Arun tapped his fingers on the table, waiting for somebody to approach him. He had been called for an emergency related to Ashwin. The message was ambiguous and urgent, forcing Arun to quit everything and come down to Delhi..

Soon, Shantanu, Mrinal, Tahir and a criminal psychologist walked in. Arun looked terrified as they introduced themselves.

"Is it some kind of interrogation? Is Ashwin alright?"

"He is fine, Mr Deb. Please sit down!" Dr Parakshit Nigam, the psychologist, spoke softly. "We have only called you for a discussion.

Based on the outcome of today's meeting, we will proceed towards a formal interrogation."

"Interrogation? What are the charges?" Arun panicked.

"Conspiring the murder of the Prime Minister of India."

"Ashwin? What nonsense!" Arun spoke indignantly. "I want to speak to him, *now!*"

"Mr Deb, your meeting will be arranged. Please cooperate with us," Mrinal said pulling a chair for Arun.

"On what basis do you suspect me? His best friend?"

"I request you to sit," Shantanu motioned at the chair and Arun sat down.

"It's a mere discussion," Dr Nigam stressed. "Please don't worry." He pressed a button on his device and began.

"Please answer my question only with a yes or no."

Arun nodded nervously.

"Do you know you are adopted?"

"Yes."

"Do you know you had a mental illness that led to violent behaviour when you were young?"

"Umm…No."

"Do you know Ashwin is adopted?"

"Yes."

"Do you know you both hail from Tamil Nadu?"

"Yes."

Dr Nigam nodded. "Now we will need slightly elaborate answers. One liners preferably." Arun nodded again.

"For how long have you been friends with Ashwin?"

"Since we were ten; thirty-six years!"

"Have you helped Ashwin in school?"

"Yes."

"Have you helped Ashwin achieve his goals?"

"As in?"

"His aspirations. From being the school prefect and holding student rallies to his political career."

"Yes"

"Have you ever told him?"

"No. There was no need to!"

"Why did you help him and never told him about it?" The doctor looked at him.

"Because he is my best friend!" Arun replied flatly.

"I agree. What doesn't connect is that you made him powerful while chose to remain a sidekick."

"Robin is pretty amazing!" Arun said jokingly. "I had similar aspirations."

"Your mother wasn't happy with the word 'sidekick' though," said Nigam curtly.

"Her opinion!" Arun replied.

"Did you ever feel Mr Jamwal was subduing you?"

"What? No!"

"What does power mean to you?"

"Control." Arun shrugged. He realized that Dr Nigam was defecting from the chain of questions rapidly to detect a sudden change in his tone and nonverbal behaviour.

"How far would you go to get power?"

"Not even till your chair."

"We are in no mood for jokes, Mr Deb. Please answer honestly or it could have very bitter consequences."

"Nowhere." Arun added in frustration. "I am not attracted to power. I am a lazy person. That's why I was happy being the sidekick and it is the same reason why I am getting interrogated here," then looking at Tahir he said, "by you!"

"So, you don't aspire to acquire power, but you could be envious of the one who has it!"

"I don't know what you are deriving at?" Arun said exasperatedly. "And how you zeroed in on my name, because of all the people in the world, I will never harm Ashwin."

"Mr Deb, Please—"

"I will cooperate. Do whatever you want. Feed me with drugs or put me in stress positions, my answers will not change."

"Mr Deb! Please listen."

"No! You listen. I can never harm Ashwin for power or for all the money in the world. I helped Ashwin because I knew, for him, acceptability to change was as difficult as it was for me. We have seen the worst of human kind. *He* has seen the worst of humanity. We both have dark abysmal pasts. Its memories torture us, follow us wherever we go. To survive, we began finding ways to escape it. Ashwin closed his eyes and moved on, refusing to believe that he was ever a part of the hell. He made goals and found missions to complete. I needed to get out from my past as well, so I made Ashwin's aspirations my own. Frankly speaking, that time I was happy to have a purpose to live. It didn't go beyond that. Never will."

♌

"I am feeling sorry for Mr Jamwal," said Mrinal

"We all are. But we don't have time to feel sorry," Tahir remarked. "Hades gave us one job and we couldn't even do that. We still don't know where and when that man will meet Mr. Jamwal."

"I *am* trying," Mrinal emphasized, hurt at the remark.

"I know you are. I am just frustrated. It's not comforting to see Mr. Jamwal broken like this," Tahir said sadly.

"And then to know your best friend could be behind your misery," Mrinal shook his head. "What could you make out from the discussion with Arun Deb?" he asked Dr Nigam, shuffling through the report.

"Like I have mentioned, Mr Deb is telling the truth. Unless…"

"Unless?"

"He is suffering from an acute mental disorder."

"That's possible?"

"Sadly, yes. Mr Arun Deb is still under suspicion."

♌

"I am getting frustrated now," Mrinal said removing his headphones. He was listening to Hades' video.

"You got nothing?" Tahir asked pacing back and forth.

"I am getting a very faint background sound." Mrinal frowned. 'But I can't make head and tail out of it."

"Amplify it!" Tahir pressed. "It's the 9th tomorrow and we are stuck."

Mrinal listened hard, after amplifying only the background sound. He could now hear a distant sound of a procession. It wasn't clear, but Mrinal caught that the faint voices were talking in a foreign language.

"Italian?" he mumbled, dazed.

"What?" Shantanu Jha asked. He was going through the transcript again.

"I think they're speaking in Italian. Listen," Mrinal said connecting his system to the speakers.

It was Italian for sure.

"Oh that explains."

"What?" Mrinal asked.

"Hades is a Roman God," Jha said.

"Hades is *Greek*," Nigam quipped.

Mrinal smirked at Jha who replied promptly, "I know Barbarik, Shikhandi, Yama. I don't think I needed to learn Greek mythology," he smiled sheepishly.

"I know Hindu mythology!" Mrinal said smiling at his boss.

"Strange," Tahir said looking at his tablet.

"That we know Greek mythology?" Mrinal asked.

"No, I wasn't even listening to you!" Tahir retorted still looking at the screen. "Adya Batra was in Italy last year, at the same time when Mr Jamwal went there for a holiday."

"She is pretty close to Mr Jamwal," Mrinal said.

"Yes, but the strange part is that she was not with him. Mr Jamwal was alone with his parents."

"Wow!"

♌

"You are scared!"

"I am not!"

"Then why are you sleeping here tonight?" Ashwin asked.

"Because you are unwell. I will ensure you rest!" Adya replied sitting next to him.

"I have slept the entire day!" Ashwin frowned.

"That's how it should be."

"A maniac has issued a death warrant for me for tomorrow and I spent my only day alive sleeping." He laughed. "I could have spent it living…with you," Ashwin said pulling her to him.

"You will," she said resting her head on his chest.

♌

Arun did not sleep. He waited for the night to pass. Arun was taken to a plush guest room at the farthest end of the PM's residence. He was told that another round of interrogation would follow, but it never did. They just locked him in that room which meant that he was still under suspicion. He had to get out of the room and meet Ashwin. He didn't have time. He had to act fast.

Arun recalled the location of Ashwin's room from his last visit and made a mental map to get there without being caught. It was close to five and morning was yet to break. He opened the window and peered into the darkness. There was no security around this part of the house anymore. He opened the window wide and sat on the sill, letting his legs hang. He remained there for a few minutes so that his brain could adapt to the height. He was at least thirteen feet from the ground.

Slowly, he turned and lowered himself. Grabbing the sill, he let his body swing, till he caught the drainage pipe with his legs. He pushed himself to the pipe, holding on to it tightly before letting his hands go off the sill. He then sluggishly lowered himself through that pipe. Once terra firma, he lay on the grass for a few minutes. These stunts were not fit for a man in his mid-forties!

He re-entered the house from the backdoor. Remembering the directions, he cautiously took the stairs and reached Ashwin's room. Ashwin wasn't there. In the faint glow of the night lamp, he saw Adya sleeping on Ashwin's bed. For a moment he thought he had come into the wrong room, but creases on the other side of the bed suggested Ashwin's presence. Arun quickly checked the bathroom. Ashwin wasn't there either.

"Damn!" he said under his breath and left hurriedly.

♌

"Oh fuck!" Mrinal said getting up suddenly. "It's close to six, we must hurry!" he began walking towards the door. The other men followed.

They saw Adya going out.

"Where is Mr Jamwal?" Jha asked

Mrinal came back from Ashwin's room and reported his absence.

Panicked, the men ran outside. They all parted ways and began calling Ashwin's name.

He wasn't in the garden. They all began moving towards the backyard.

Finally they spotted Ashwin. He was on the ground, gasping for breath. Arun was standing opposite him with a gun in his hands. He threw the gun and knelt before him. Ashwin's left abdomen was bleeding profusely. Adya was standing a few feet from them.

"He killed him!" she cried, her body going limp. Mrinal held her and continued walking. "You guys never listened to me!" Adya refused to walk further. "Arun killed him!" she wailed.

Mrinal left her and rushed towards the site.

"Arun did not kill Ashwin!" Tahir said from behind and Adya shot him a glance.

"He is alive," declared Mrinal. "No significant damage either."

"So he *tried* to kill Ashwin," Adya found her voice back.

"He didn't *try* to kill Ashwin. He saved him!"

"What? From whom?" Adya asked surprised.

"From himself, ma'am," Tahir replied softly. "Mr Ashwin Jamwal is Hades!"

It was eight in the morning. Tahir, Mrinal, Shantanu Jha, Arun and Dr Nigam waited anxiously in the living room for Adya to join them. Ashwin was being treated by some reputed doctors. For obvious reasons, these men consciously decided to avoid hospitalization.

"The doctor said that Ashwin is out of danger," Adya said as she entered the room. "It's still hard to believe that Ashwin is a schizophrenic," she said taking her seat. "He is the most genuine person I have met and I am intrigued to find out how it all started."

"We have been arranging bits and pieces of the information to come up with the plausible back-story of Mr Jamwal and Hades," Tahir said wearily. "Dr Parikshit can tell you better."

Adya looked at the psychologist and he began.

"Mr Jamwal was born in Tamil Nadu to a poor family. We couldn't gather much information about them, so we don't know how he ended up in a firework factory at the young age of six. Either his parents forced him into labour, or they sold him to the company, we will never know." He stopped as Adya gasped. "Terrible things happen, Ms Adya," he said and then continued. "After a few months, he was rescued, along with other children by the Sri Mataji Trust. They brought him, and Mr Deb – an orphan and a child labour at a small idly shop – to Indore, because they both were fair, which made them victims of physical and sexual abuse in the Tamil Nadu Centre."

Arun gulped. "I didn't know Ashwin before the adoption; we both were in different branches. How did we end up getting adopted on the same day?"

"Mr and Mrs Jamwal did not have a child after ten years of marriage. Mrs Jamwal's best friend, Mrs Deb, lost her son to pneumonia when he was twenty-eight months old."

"Is it?" Arun asked. His parents had never told him.

"Yes," replied the doctor. "Mrs Jamwal was a strong idealistic woman; she decided to adopt a child in need and persuaded Mrs Deb to do so as well. Mrs. Jamwal knew someone at the Sri Mataji trust and contacted them. Finally, on the same date, both the families adopted two boys, who were of the same age as their child would have been."

"But then, why do we celebrate different birthdays?" Arun asked

"Your parents celebrate your real birthday; while his parents celebrated the adoption date as his birthday," Tahir replied.

"So I was saying," Dr Parikshit continued, "While Mr Deb had trouble forgetting his past and adjusting to the new environment, Mr Jamwal shut himself from his past and accepted his new family as his real family. That was his way of escapism, but it didn't work. Those horrifying memories from his past remained, buried deep in his subconscious. He was the victim of a cruel social system. He must have seen unjust treatment of the society favouring powerful people. At some point, he must have wanted to fight, to retaliate, but couldn't, because he was nothing. That feeling to rise above everyone else led to the making of his alter ego, Hades."

"That's why Ashwin made such a diabolical plan?" Adya asked.

"Not *Mr Jamwal*, Hades. Please understand Hades and Ashwin are two different people. A modern day Dr Jekyll and Mr Hyde. Hades was least like Mr Jamwal. He was at least twenty years older than Mr Jamwal."

"Hades? A strange name! I never knew it co-existed with Ashwin," Arun said baffled. "How and when did Hades appear? Why could the people close to Ashwin never notice anything unusual?"

"Hades may be an uncommon name in India, finding its place only in video games and so on. It wasn't so rare for Ashwin who was brought up by a family interested in world art and culture. For all we know, he must have read *The Iliad* at a very young age!" Nigam said drinking his tea.

"Yes! He is well read and well-travelled." Arun smiled. "You remember he used to bring souvenirs from his international trips?" he asked Adya.

"Yes! He used to travel twice or thrice every year. His mother's family lives in Europe." Adya smiled. "Arun is right, how did we never notice Hades?"

"Because Hades never came out in the open. Schizophrenia fades with age, if treated properly, but that didn't happen in Mr Jamwal's case, because Hades used to work covertly. That's why nobody saw him. That's how it was meant to be! His mother had talked about his 'social closures' wherein he would not talk to anyone for days. That was Hades taking over. And Ashwin's parents linked it with the emotional turmoil due to his past," Dr Nigam said. "Hades started controlling events around Mr Jamwal, and facilitated his entry into politics." He paused as if he remembered something.

"Let me remind you, while Mr Jamwal was in his twenties, Hades must have been above fifty. He acted and behaved like a fifty-year-old. He knew the right people and he knew how to carry out operations which a normal young man could not even think of. He was good at computers and technology, while Mr Jamwal is rather technologically challenged." Adya smiled, she knew how Ashwin struggled when he got a new phone or tablet.

"Hades started to operate through local goons and had gradually built a strong international network. He was the key middleman in illicit energy and ammunition trading across the globe." Dr Parikshit said taking his seat. "It wasn't difficult for him as it happened when online transition was in its initial stages, and people were less secure. He used his knowledge of hacking and computer programming to get the deepest information. He sold it slowly; from just a seller of information to one, party he became intermediary, drawing profits from both parties."

"He is very rich," Mrinal said pleasantly.

"Why did he need money?" Arun asked.

"To carry out his master plan!" the psychologist replied. "A plan, as devious as this, requires years to fructify. Hades must have thought about it twenty years back and since then, whatever he did, he did only to make this day happen."

Adya gasped. "How did you find about it?"

"The first lead was in the video which he shared with you!" Mrinal replied. "Initially we missed the obvious," Mrinal rubbed his eyes in exhaustion. "But after amplifying the sounds in the video, enough till we could hear a distant faint sound of chants and music. We dug further and found that it was the sound of some Italian festival... something *terza...*" he shook his head.

"Terzieri Palio," Tahir helped him

"Yes, Terzie... Anyway, it is celebrated in a town called Montecassiano. It's a small town and it was not difficult to locate the direction of the sound, which was thirty degrees west from the room where the recording happened. It was the same hotel where Mr Ashwin Jamwal was staying with his parents at that time. We also discovered that you were in Italy during that time."

"Initially we thought it's you," Tahir said looking at Adya.

"Me?"

"You were in Ancona during that time, only one hour away!"

"Yes." Adya thought hard, "I didn't know Ashwin was spending his vacation there, though. I went there for a friend's wedding."

"We know," Tahir replied solemnly. "That gave us one lead – Hades was someone close to Ashwin who knew about his whereabouts. So we started going through all the images and videos of the vacation that Mrs. Jamwal shared with us. What we found shocked us."

"What?"

"We spotted Mr. Ashwin in some of the images as a tourist." Dr Nigam added, "He was alone at a distance and not part of the actual shot. We spoke to his mother and found out that Ashwin had refused to go with them that day as he had a migraine attack!"

"He suffers from migraines," Adya said.

"It wasn't migraine!" Dr Nigam said. "It was his brain chemicals reacting to the sudden transition from Ashwin to Hades."

"Mr. Jamwal never goes to a tourist location alone; that behaviour was very unlike him, so I decided to check his schedule for that day. There was nothing relevant. Alarmed, I got into Mr Jamwal's personal system – his tablets and a laptop."

"He doesn't use a laptop anymore. He uses tablets!" Arun frowned.

"Precisely!" Mrinal added. "But he has an old laptop which he never discarded! This also accentuated Dr Nigam's theory that some part of his brain restricted him to throw away the laptop." Mrinal shrugged. "We found some hidden files in that system with cryptic codes and messages. We got a crypto-analyst and a whole new world of Hades opened before us!"

"The analyst said that the codes were pretty easy to decipher," Tahir said grimly, "As though Hades wanted somebody to decode them."

"Hades was really proud of his actions, just like some Nazi soldiers who voice recorded their merciless killings during the holocaust," Dr Nigam added. "He wanted people to find out how he had designed the whole plan."

"He had a group of trusted aides, who helped him without revealing his identity. Zahan, the man RAW got in El Sal, was one of them. There are more, we will trace them," Mrinal concluded.

"He must have befriended Ivan – the vindictive and frustrated KGB officer and the alleged mastermind of the WMD attack," Tahir continued. "Hades supported him financially and facilitated the operations. Hades had resources! His people were fanatics from across the globe. Like you said, Mr Jamwal had travelled a lot; he must have seen lots of people with pain and hatred against the system. Ashwin would have ignored them, but Hades saw the hatred and somehow contacted them; looping them into his master plan. All the men in his team had an agenda. Hades helped them achieve that and in a way, he was benefitted in the end! He had people working for him in India as well!"

"What did he do in India?" Arun frowned.

"Well, till now we found that he was responsible for the death of former Cabinet Minister A.K. Nandi, his mistress of sorts Sumona Thandi and I.M. Raathi!"

"Raathi's suicide was hard to believe. I am sad to know that Ashwin was behind it."

"It's Hades, Mr Deb," Mrinal stressed. "Coming back to his modus operandi, since he was tech savvy, he always remained a step ahead of his enemies by hacking their communicating devices and bugging their surroundings. We found that he attacks his enemies when the enemy is most comfortable. On a date and in a place very closely related to them. Raathi died on the date he had formed the Nationalistic Party, Nandi on his birthday, Sumona on the date she became the owner of the Thandi group. It was natural that Hades would attack Ashwin on his birthday, at his place and at the time when he was born." He looked at Arun and asked, "How did you end up at the scene?"

"I just wanted to see Ashwin desperately. When I didn't find him in his bedroom, I started looking for him. I saw him walking in the backyard and followed him," Arun paused. "I called out to him, but he was talking to himself. I rushed to his side and touched his shoulders. His eyes were bloodshot and were that of a stranger. He didn't seem to know me. He pulled out a gun and aimed it at me. He said something like 'I am about to meet my destiny. Fuck off or else I will kill you'. That's when he heard Adya from behind."

"And then us. He pointed the gun at himself," Dr Nigam said leaning over the sofa.

"Yes. I tried to stop him, but he fired."

"Otherwise he would have definitely killed you before killing himself. When he heard us, he feared his mission could be delayed further. He didn't want that!'

"Glad that gun had a silencer, otherwise the news would have reached the media," Arun said quietly.

"But what now?" asked Adya anxiously.

"As such, he has made up his mind to resign. After he is fit physically, he will undergo therapy. He will be fine," Dr Nigam said simply.

"What about his offences? What are the charges?"

Four government officers exchanged glances. Tahir spoke.

"There are no charges. Ivan Kuruserv has taken responsibility for the attack."

"But Ashwin helped him. He is the mastermind," Adya said looking confused.

"Hades, not Ashwin!" Nigam corrected her.

"We cannot persecute Mr Jamwal for crimes his alter ego committed," Tahir said softly. "The laws of the land, for split personality, are very evasive and we personally feel it would be unfair for Mr Jamwal to face consequences of Hades's actions. So, we have decided to bury it. This place has buried many secrets in the past. Let this be one of those. Mr Jamwal is a phenomenon. He has given Indians a reason to stand tall and hope. If this comes out in public, people will again fall into oblivion; never believing in their leaders again. The people deserve to live with a hope that a leader like Mr Jamwal will emerge and change India for the better."

Epilogue

"It is good to see you like a normal happy person," Arun told Ashwin.

Arun was at a cafe in London with Adya and Ashwin. Almost two years had passed since Ashwin resigned as the Prime Minister. After spending a good amount of time in therapy, Ashwin settled in London with Adya and started writing a book. They were planning to get married and had invited Arun to share the news with him.

"How is the transition from Prime Minister to writer going?" Arun asked sipping his coffee.

"To be honest, I feel he has always been a writer," Adya replied.

"I also feel I have been always been a writer," Ashwin smiled and then added softly. "Also, I am not proud of whatever happened. It is still hard to believe that I had an alter ego...who...who was an international criminal. I get very restless sometimes. It is killing me inside. I sometimes feel like going out into the open and owning up to my actions. But then what actions? I do not remember doing anything!"

"Because you didn't do it! Don't let this spoil the time you have," Arun said pleasantly.

"What if he still exists? How would I know?" Ashwin asked.

"He doesn't!" Adya said rubbing Ashwin's arms. "You're cured and you go for regular checkups. You get crazy philosophical sometimes, but there is no Hades!" Everyone laughed.

"How do you even tolerate him?" Arun joked.

"I often wonder." Ashwin laughed. "There won't be any escape for her after we are married."

"Ashwin!" Adya said, "We were supposed to surprise him!"

"Finally! At the age of fifty, you both decided to get married!" Arun laughed and hugged Ashwin.

♌

The day ended well for Justin, the waiting staff of the cafe. Not only did he see his favourite customers behaving like college students, he also got a huge tip from them. Ashwin and Adya were regulars in the restaurant. Justin knew that Ashwin Jamwal was the PM of India a few years back and he was honoured to wait his table. In the last one year, he had built a special bond with them.

Back home, Justin looked at his tip and as a habit kept it in the iron box, not knowing what to do with it anymore. Earlier he used to save all his money only to send it to his poor family in the Philippines. Ten years ago, a political unrest led to the annihilation of his entire village. Except for his sixteen-year-old sister, his entire family was killed. He rushed home hoping to find his dear sister, but after months of searching, he found her warped body lying with ten other such cadavers in a paddy field. He was told that armed men had raped young girls in the streets. When the body of the girl couldn't take any more, they would just stab her to death.

Ten years had passed. He had just accepted his fate; he had not been able to do anything then, he couldn't do anything now, except to live with an indelible pain. A pain which he hid behind his perpetual smile. He switched on his tablet to watch a customary B-grade movie before sleeping. He was in the middle of it when he received a video conference request. Confused, he accepted it.

His screen went dark and he heard a man's voice.

Hades.